Susan Gates
Valentine's Day
1966

The Happy Hollisters and the Mystery of the Golden Witch

BY JERRY WEST

Illustrated by Helen S. Hamilton

GARDEN CITY, NEW YORK

Doubleday & Company, Inc.

Contents

CHAPTER 1

RUNAWAY PUMPKINS

"PUMPKINS—goodie!" exclaimed four-year-old Sue Hollister. "I love Halloween!" The little girl bounced on the back seat of the station wagon as the family drove toward Mr. Johnson's farm.

Beside her squirmed pig-tailed Holly, who was six. She put both pinkies into her mouth and stretched the corners.

"Oh, Holly, don't," pleaded Pam. "Your face might *stay* that way!"

"She looks like a jack-o'-lantern anyhow," sighed redheaded Ricky, who was seven. He added, "Yikes! How many are we going to get?"

"One pumpkin for each of us," said Pete hopefully. He was twelve, two years older than Pam, and sat in the front seat between his mother and his father, who was driving.

As they neared the farm not far from their home in Shoreham, Pam suddenly gasped and cried, "Daddy, look out!" Three big pumpkins came rolling down a lane into the road.

Thud! Thump! Splat! They hit the station wagon and were smashed to smithereens.

5

Mr. Hollister pulled to the side of the road, stopped the car, and they all got out. Pieces of pumpkin were stuck on the front bumper, and the front right wheel was smeared with pumpkin seeds. The fender, too, had been hit, but there was only a small dent on it, which could hardly be seen.

Carefully watching the Sunday-afternoon traffic, Pete and Pam hastened into the road and removed the pieces of slippery pumpkin.

"What made the pumpkins run away?" asked Sue, tugging at her mother's hand. Mrs. Hollister, a pretty, slender woman smiled at her daughter and said, "Maybe they didn't want to be made into jack-o'-lanterns. Perhaps Daddy knows why."

Mr. Hollister was a tall athletic-looking man with a pleasant smile. He had already taken a cloth from inside the car and had wiped everything clean. "The lane the pumpkins rolled out of is on Mr. Johnson's farm," he said. "Come on, let's see what's the matter."

The mother and father and five youngsters walked back toward the lane. They were a happy family and often shared mystery and adventure together. Sometimes their travels took them to distant places, but now and then they met with mysteries right in their home town. Shoreham was located on beautiful Pine Lake, and the Hollisters' big comfortable house was situated on the shore of the lake a mile or so from Mr. Johnson's farm. They had come there to buy pumpkins to be used in making jack-o'-lanterns for a Halloween party the children were planning to have.

When they reached the lane, they turned in. It was narrow and stony, leading up a small hill. Blond, fluffy-haired Pam took Sue's hand and helped her climb.

Pete ran on ahead. He turned, gestured with his arm, and called out, "I see what's the trouble."

"What is it?" Ricky asked, dashing to his side.

"There's a tractor in the ditch up ahead."

"Yikes!" Ricky exclaimed. "And a wagonload of pumpkins has turned over."

All five youngsters hurried on ahead, and reached the scene shortly before their parents.

Farmer Johnson, a middle-aged man with a weatherbeaten face, looked up from the ditch where he was surveying the damage to his tractor.

"Hello, Mr. Johnson," the children's father called out. "What's your trouble?"

The man removed a cap, mopped his brow, and climbed onto the road. "Broken axle," he said. "My tractor skidded into the ditch and look what happened to my load of pumpkins."

"Three of them rolled down the road and banged into us!" Holly declared, twirling one of her brown pigtails.

"I hope no one was hurt," Mr. Johnson said quickly.

"Our car looked like a pumpkin pie for a few minutes, but it's all right now," said Pam. She tried to make a joke so that their farmer friend would not feel so bad.

But the man did not smile. He looked sorrowfully at the tractor and the spilled load of pumpkins.

"Trouble and more trouble," he said with a sigh, and thrust his hands deep into his overall pockets. "First my farm helper leaves just in the middle of harvest, and now this!"

"Can't you get another one?" Ricky asked.

"I've tried," Mr. Johnson replied, "but there's a shortage of workers this fall. I'll have to do without a farmhand, all right, and that's no joke."

"Maybe we can help you," Pete said.

Now a little smile flicked across Farmer Johnson's face. "You're nice to say that, Pete," he said. "But how?"

The boy ran his hand over his blond crew-cut hair. "Well, first of all, we can set the wagon upright and gather these pumpkins."

"Good idea, Pete," said Mr. Hollister. "Let's get started." He jumped into the ditch and helped the farmer uncouple the wagon shaft from a hitch that connected it to the back of the tractor; then, with everyone pitching in, the wagon was pulled out of the ditch and onto the lane. As Mrs. Hollister set a stone behind the back wheels, her family began to gather the pumpkins that had rolled into the nearby field. Even dark-haired Sue, giggling with delight, carried the smallest pumpkins to the wagon.

"Ricky, Pete, come over here!" called their father. "I need help with this one!" Together the three lifted a huge golden-yellow globe and half stumbling, carried it to the wagon.

"All ready, now, one, two, three—heave!" said Mr. Hollister, and the pumpkin rolled onto the floor of the wagon. The red-cheeked boys took a deep breath of crisp October air.

"Yikes," said Ricky, "what a monster!"

The farmer glanced up at the setting sun, which slanted brightly over the farm. "If you'll excuse me, I'll hurry on ahead," he said. "I have to phone for a mechanic to get here before dark."

"I hope you can find one on Sunday afternoon," said Mr. Hollister, and added, "We'll pull the wagon to the barn for you."

"Yikes! I like to play horse!" exclaimed Ricky as he grabbed the wagon shaft.

Pete, Pam and Mr. Hollister pulled on it also, while Mrs. Hollister and the other children pushed from the rear. With creaking wheels, the wagon went up the hill, around a bend, and along a level stretch which led to Mr. Johnson's barn and beyond it the rambling farmhouse. On the way they passed a grove of willow trees with long, yellow leaves. Beside it was a little duck pond, fed by a narrow stream that trickled down the hillside. In a field nearby were tethered three small goats on long chains.

When the Hollisters reached the barn, Holly dashed over to a wire enclosure at the side of it. "Look!" she cried. "Chickens!" As she stooped,

"Yikes! I like to play horse!"

clucking at the hens, Mr. Johnson and his wife approached, smiling.

"Thank you for helping us!" said Mrs. Johnson. She was tall and thin with dark hair pulled tightly into a bun. Holly ran up to her and the farm woman put an arm around her. "I was making pumpkin pies when my husband told me of his troubles," she said. Then, with a big sigh she added, "I don't know what we'll do now with all the pumpkins to harvest and no tractor or horse to pull the wagon."

"That's the trouble with a tractor," the farmer said with a wry smile. "They sometimes break."

"But horses don't break, do they?" chirped little Sue. When she said this, a bright look came into Pete's face.

"Crickets! I have an idea!" he said. "Why don't we lend Domingo to Mr. Johnson? He can help to pull the pumpkins from the field."

"Domingo's our burro," Holly put in quickly.

"I've got a better idea," said Pam. "Why don't we *all* help Mr. and Mrs. Johnson."

"Like after school, you mean?" asked Ricky. "Yikes! That would be great!"

The grownups exchanged amused glances and Pam said, "Really, we mean it."

"That will be fine," said Mr. Johnson, "and, of course, I'll pay you."

"We wouldn't think of it," declared Pete.

Ricky was so excited that he did a cartwheel on the grass and out of his jacket pocket fell a penknife, a plastic whistle, a long nail, and two pennies.

Quickly scooping up his treasures, he dashed toward the wooded hillside that sloped up some distance behind the barn. "Come on, let's play hide-and-seek!" he cried out.

Ricky raced ahead to the edge of the woods, turned, and ran back even faster. "Mr. Johnson!" he called. "Is that another barn back there?" He pointed to an old building with a caved-in roof. It was nearly concealed by tall saplings, whose thinning leaves had turned to red and gold.

"You've never noticed that before?" the farmer asked, his eyes twinkling at the boy's curiosity.

"No."

"Neither have I," said Pete. "In summer the leaves from the trees hide it, I guess."

Mr. Johnson explained that the tumbledown barn, surrounded by weeds and brush, had been falling into decay for many years.

His wife spoke up. "We don't even go back there any more," she said.

"Come on, let's explore it," suggested tomboy Holly.

But before the youngsters could take one step, a weird sound came from the ramshackle barn.

Oo-ga, oo-ga.

"What was that?" exclaimed Pam.

Ricky laughed. "It's a Halloween spook! I'll bet Mr. Johnson is playing a trick on us."

But the farmer frowned. "That's no trick," he said. With long and determined strides, he headed toward the ruined barn.

As the Hollisters hurried along behind him, Ricky whispered to his brother, "Yikes, another mystery, Pete! Isn't this great!"

"Maybe it's no mystery at all," the older boy replied. They pushed their way through the tall weeds and came up to the barn door. The wood was rotted and one of the hinges had rusted through, leaving the door askew.

Pam shuddered. "It looks like a broken bat's wing," she said. As they stepped into the gloomy interior, a musty smell greeted them. Peering around in the half-light, they saw the caved-in roof resting atop several horse stalls and a rickety ladder leading to a loft where moldy hay peeked out like stiff, unruly hair.

Off in one corner Pete could make out something with wheels on it. Cautiously he walked across the barn floor and then cried out, "Look, an old car."

Mr. Hollister came close on his heels and said with a chuckle, "It's a model-T Ford, a Tin Lizzie."

"Yup, that's what we used to call 'em," said the farmer. Dust hung thick on all parts of the old touring car. The top had been removed many years before, and the wheels were raised off the floor by four wooden blocks under the axles.

"But look here," said Pam. Near the left-hand door was fastened an ancient horn. A push knob on top of it was free of dust. Pam put her hand on it and a throaty growl came from the horn.

"Haven't seen a klaxon like that in years!" exclaimed Mr. Hollister. He pressed hard.

Oo-ga, oo-ga. The loud noise filled the barn.

"That's what it was! That's where the sound came from!" said Ricky.

"But who could have honked the horn?" Mrs. Hollister asked. All eyes peered about the barn, searching out every corner where someone might be hiding. There was no one inside.

"This is a real Halloween mystery," declared Mrs. Johnson.

"Who owns this old car, Mr. Johnson?" asked Pete.

"I do," came the reply. "It belonged to the former owner of this place and was left here when I bought the farm."

Pete glanced at the car fondly but said nothing more. Then Ricky spoke up. "Yikes, this would be a great place to hold a spooky Halloween party."

"It's spooky, all right," said Pam, as she wiped a cobweb from her forehead. "But it's too dirty in here."

"If you children are looking for a place to have a party," the farmer said, as he led them out of the old building, "why not use my new barn? You'll have lots of room there."

"Could we really?" asked Pam.

"Sure, that's how I can pay you for helping me," he said.

The Hollister children were delighted with the offer. As they skipped back toward the farmhouse, Sue raced ahead into some high weeds. Suddenly she screamed and disappeared from sight!

CHAPTER 2

A TREASURE CLUE

PAM dashed into the weeds toward the spot where Sue had vanished. Suddenly she came upon her small sister lying face down and crying. She had tripped over a low railing.

"Ow!" she cried, as Pam helped her to her feet.

"Goodness, what happened?" Mrs. Hollister asked, running up to them. She looked at the iron railing, hidden by the leaves, which surrounded a rectangular plot of ground. The rest of the family came hurrying up behind her with Farmer Johnson and his wife.

"What is this, anyhow?" asked Ricky, as he started to do a balancing act on the rusty old rail.

"This is a private graveyard," Mr. Johnson replied.

"So it is!" said Pete, pushing his way through the tall brown grass to a nearly hidden headstone.

As he parted the weeds to get a better look at it, Mrs. Johnson told them that many farms in the old days had private burying places.

16

Pam joined Pete as he knelt down to read an inscription cut into the stone. It said:

ADAM CORNWALL
WHO READS MY STONE AND DROPS A TEER
MAY FIND A TRESURE IN THE AIRE

After Pete had read it aloud, Ricky pressed forward to look at the stone and said, "Ha-ha, somebody couldn't spell!"

"Look who's talking," Holly said and Ricky grinned. Then she added brightly, "Sue ought to find the treasure because she's the one who's crying."

Pam looked up at the farmer. "What can this verse mean, Mr. Johnson?" she asked.

"I don't know," he replied, as his wife shook her head, puzzled.

Suddenly Sue cried, "I see it!" She dashed off, made a quick darting motion with her hand, and returned with a big yellow moth. "This is the treasure I found in the air," she said.

"Oh, Sue," said Pam, "let the poor thing go."

The little girl parted her chubby fingers, and away the moth zigzagged through the autumn air. She watched it happily, her face still wet with tears.

Farmer Johnson said that there had been several smaller gravestones on the plot when he bought the farm but that curiosity-hunters had made off with them.

"Do you really think we have found another mystery to solve?" Pam asked, as they walked back toward the new barn.

Mrs. Hollister nodded and Pete said, "Of course we have! Isn't there some kind of a prowler around here? And now the promise of a treasure in the air."

Mr. Hollister winked at his wife, then looked up into the deepening blue sky. "The air is a pretty big place," he said. "You might look forever to find a treasure up there."

In front of the barn stood several rows of baskets filled with red apples. "Those are from my orchard," the farmer said, pointing to a grove of trees at the end of his property. "How would you children like some cider?"

"Thank you," said Pam. "We'd love it."

As the Hollisters followed the farmer and his wife to the rear door of their home, Mr. Johnson told them that he used some of his own apples to make cider. They were pressed at Aunt Nettie's Cider Mill, which was located over the hill. He stopped to point at the dark woods rising on the slope behind his farm. "There's an old cart road," he said, "which leads directly to the cider mill."

"Maybe we could cart your apples there," Pete said. He told the Johnsons that they had a two-wheel cart, which their burro, Domingo, sometimes pulled.

"Good," the farmer said. "I'll have a load ready for you Thursday."

"Great!" Pete replied. "We'll come right after school."

They all filed into the big kitchen of the farmhouse, where Mrs. Johnson poured them tall glasses of delicious brown apple cider.

While the others were busy talking, Pam sipped her drink and gazed out the window toward the edge of the woods. Suddenly she set her glass down and squeezed Pete's arm. "Look over there," she whispered. Pete, too, looked out the window in time to see a young woman at the edge of the woods. She wore a red jacket with a yellow design on the back of it. Glancing around nervously, she walked swiftly toward the old barn.

Could she be the mysterious prowler? Unnoticed by the others, Pete and Pam slipped out the back door in time to see her disappear into the trees in front of the old barn.

"Come on!" exclaimed Pete, and sprinted across the farmyard with Pam at his heels. When they reached the fringe of the woods, they stopped, then tiptoed up to the side of the ramshackle building. Pete pressed his ear against a crack between the boards. Something was moving inside!

A moment later the door creaked. The children peered around the corner and saw the red-jacketed figure come out and hurry away. Pete and Pam followed quietly and saw the strange girl step over the rail into the graveyard. With her back to them, she began sweeping the weeds aside and

Something was moving inside!

scanning the ground. Suddenly she straightened up and stood looking into the woods.

"Hello," Pete called. "We'd like to talk to you." The girl glanced back, surprised, then dashed off into the woods. "Crickets," said Pete, "she certainly acted odd."

"She seemed to be searching for something," Pam remarked. "Maybe it was a clue to the treasure."

When they reached the farmhouse and told their story, Ricky asked what the girl looked like.

"She had brown hair," Pete replied, "but we didn't get a good look at her face."

"Do you think she's the one who sounded the horn on the old car?" Holly asked.

"Could be," replied Pete. "When we start to help Mr. Johnson tomorrow, we'll keep a lookout for her."

Mrs. Johnson smiled. "So you'll be detectives as well as farm helpers."

"I think we're very lucky you Hollisters came over today," declared her husband.

"And now we'll buy a few pumpkins to take home with us," Mr. Hollister said, as he reached for his wallet.

"We wouldn't think of it," said Mrs. Johnson. "You help yourself to all the pumpkins you want."

Each of the children went to the wagon and chose a pumpkin for making a jack-o'-lantern. They thanked the Johnsons, then walked to their car, put the big orange fruit into the back, and set off for home.

After supper, Mr. Hollister asked the four older children to take the pumpkins out of the car and put them in the garage. "That's a cool place and they'll keep well there until it's time to carve them," he said.

The youngsters trooped into the garage, which was a large frame building. They lined up the fruit neatly against a wall, and all left except Pete. He went over to one side where their burro stood in his stall.

"Hi, Domingo," Pete said, scratching the animal's ears. The pet lifted his head and let out, "Ee-aw."

"How would you like to work on a farm?" Pete asked. The burro gave the same answer.

"Good boy," said Pete. He hastened into the house and declared, "I just talked to Domingo about his new job and he says it's all right."

"We heard him," said Holly, wrinkling her nose. "And we'd better take Zip too."

Zip was the Hollisters' beautiful collie. In addition to this golden-coated dog they also had six cats. Whitenose was the mother, and she had five kittens: Midnight, Snow Ball, Smoky, Tutti-Frutti, and Cuddly. Their home was a carton in the basement.

Little Sue switched on the light, descended the basement steps, and petted each of the fluffy kittens, before saying good night and going to bed.

Next morning on the way to school, Pete, Pam, Ricky, and Holly told their friends about the new mystery they had discovered.

"Oh, I hope you find out what the treasure is," said Ann Hunter, Pam's best friend. She was ten years old and had dark curly hair. Her gray eyes sparkled with excitement as she added, "If you need any help, you know we're ready."

She was referring to a detective club that the Hollisters had formed some time before.

"Okay," said Pam brightly as they walked into the school yard. "This may be a mystery where we'll need *everybody* to help."

It was hard for Pete, especially, to keep his mind on the lessons that day. He was glad when the final bell rang and he hastened home to hitch Domingo to the cart.

As Pete ran into the driveway with his books, he stopped short at the sight before him. The garage door was open and the two-wheel cart was standing before it. From the garage came Ricky leading Domingo. "How did you get home ahead of me?" Pete asked.

"My teacher gave me a ride," Ricky replied. "I told her that I had to work on a farm, and I needed to get started right away."

"You shouldn't have done that," said his brother.

"She was glad to drop me off," Ricky said as he backed the burro between the shafts lying on the ground. "She has to pass here, anyway."

Pete chuckled as he helped the young redhead hitch Domingo.

"Here come the others now," Ricky said.

Pam and Holly flew into the yard and up the steps to put their books in the house. Pete followed with his.

"May we take Sue along?" Pam asked.

"Of course, but be careful of her," Mrs. Hollister cautioned.

Warmly dressed, the youngsters set out for their jobs on Mr. Johnson's farm. Ricky took the reins of the donkey cart. Pam, Holly, and Sue sat behind him while Pete walked beside the wagon. They started out of the driveway and along the road. *Clippity-clop, clippity-clop*, went Domingo's hoofs on the pavement. The children's faces glowed with excitement. They had gone only a quarter of a mile when, suddenly, two boys appeared on their bicycles.

"Ugh!" said Holly. "Here come Joey and Will."

Joey Brill was twelve, but big for his age, and Will Wilson was his pal. Joey, especially, was jealous of the Hollisters and the fun they had. He sometimes bullied the younger children and often tried to play mean tricks on the Hollisters.

Joey set his brake and squealed to a stop by the wagon.

"Ha, the Hollisters are moving away!" he said.

"Now wouldn't that be great," said Will.

"Where are you going?" asked Joey.

"On an errand," said Pete, without stopping.

"Come on, gee-up, Domingo," urged Ricky.

"We're going to help a farmer!" Sue blurted out.

"Yes, we're going to gather pumpkins!" Holly added.

"Pumpkins. Phooey! Who cares about pumpkins?" said Joey. He started his bicycle again. When he was abreast of the cart once more, he stopped and reached over to pick up a broken branch beside the road.

"Come on, hurry, Domingo," said Ricky, slapping the reins lightly against the burro.

With a sudden move, Joey thrust the branch into the spokes of the cart wheel. It came to an abrupt stop.

"Hey!" cried Ricky, as he pitched forward out of the cart.

CHAPTER 3

FAKE MONEY

RICKY sprawled headlong over Domingo's back
and tumbled into the street. As he picked himself
up, he rubbed his nose gingerly and Pam noticed
it was scraped. Joey and Will, meanwhile, had
pedaled off, but Pete had raced after them, grabbed
the rear mudguard of Joey's bike, and pulled the
bully to a stop.

"Let go!" cried Joey, trying to shake loose from
Pete's strong grip. Just then, Zip came bounding
along the road. Seeing the fracas between the two
boys, the collie began to bark loudly.

"Get off your bike, Joey!" Pete said, "and I'll
punch you."

"Oh, yeah? And have your dog bite me?"

"Zip won't hurt you."

"I'll fight you some other place, but not here,"
Joey protested.

Above the bark of the dog and the shouts of
the two boys, Sue's little voice sang out, "Joey's
afraid of my brother."

26

"No, I am not!" He gave his bike another hard jerk and wrenched free from Pete's grasp.

"Let him go," Pam pleaded, "otherwise we'll be late for Farmer Johnson's."

Joey scowled over his shoulder and pedaled his bike hard to join Will who had stopped halfway down the block.

"I think we'd better go home and have Mother fix Ricky's nose," said Holly, putting her face close to Ricky's freckled one for a better look at the injury.

"Yikes, it doesn't hurt much now," Ricky said. "Come on, I want to haul some pumpkins." He climbed into the cart and picked up the reins as Holly boosted Zip in. Then Ricky urged Domingo into a quick trot and away they went toward the Johnson farm.

"I feel much better with Zip guarding us," said Holly, as they passed the lane where the pumpkin collision had happened.

Soon they were at the main entrance to the farm. Ricky urged Domingo up a drive next to a roadside stand. He halted the burro in back of the farmhouse and they all got out.

Mrs. Johnson came out to greet them. When she saw Ricky's skinned nose and heard the story of the accident, she took the boy by the hand and led him into the house. There she washed his face and applied a thin adhesive bandage to the sore spot.

When Ricky joined the others, he wore the

strip on his nose proudly and Holly said, "You look like a hero, Ricky."

"I want a bandage, too," said Sue. So Mrs. Johnson got another strip, this one smaller, and put it on Sue's nose. The little girl was so happy that she reached up and kissed the farmer's wife.

Mrs. Johnson said her husband had taken some chickens to the market, then pointed out a field of pumpkins. "Some of those must be hauled to the roadstand," she said, "and we have to make a great big jack-o'-lantern as an advertisement."

"Oh, I can help you do that," Holly said.

"Good," Mrs. Johnson replied, smiling. "Suppose you and Sue stay with me while the others gather the pumpkins."

As the three older children drove the burro across to the field, the two younger girls went into the farm kitchen, where a large pumpkin sat on the table. With a stubby pencil, Holly carefully drew a triangle nose, two big eyes, and a grinning mouth on the shell. Then Mrs. Johnson cut a circle around the stem and all three took turns at hollowing out the inside with big spoons.

After the face had been carved, Mrs. Johnson said, "How about making this an extra-special pumpkin?"

"How?" asked Holly.

The woman disappeared into her pantry and returned with a stubby-looking carrot, one large red pepper, and a handful of parsley. As the youngsters giggled, she gave the jack-o'-lantern a carrot nose.

"Oh, I know what the pepper is for," sang Holly. "Ears."

"That's right," the woman said, and split the pepper. Then, with long toothpicks, she fitted the ears onto the pumpkin. "And now he shall have some hair," she said, finally, and arranged the parsley around the pumpkin's head.

By the time they had carried the jack-o'-lantern down the drive and placed it on a box beside the roadstand, Pete, Pam, and Ricky had arrived with their first load of pumpkins. They arranged them neatly on the ground, with the smaller fruit in the front and the larger ones behind. As they were doing this, an auto stopped and a man and woman stepped out.

"Oh, what a grand Halloween pumpkin!" the woman exclaimed. Turning to her husband she added, "George, don't you think we could make one just like this?"

The man nodded, grinning, and picked up a large pumpkin.

"That's a dollar-size one," Mrs. Johnson said, and took the bill which the man offered her.

"Hurray! We're doing a big business!" declared Ricky. He hopped back into the cart and set off for the field again, with Pete and Pam chasing along beside him.

"Let's get a bigger load this time," Pete said. He glanced back to see two more cars stopping at the roadstand. "Crickets, we're going to need pumpkins real fast!"

As Domingo stood by patiently, the children gathered the fruit from the withering vines and loaded them into the cart.

"Yikes," Ricky said. "Do you remember the time Daddy stood on the back step of this cart and lifted Domingo right into the air?"

"That was funny," said Pam.

"Well, let's do it again," suggested Ricky, as he lifted two pumpkins from the ground by their stems.

"What do you mean?" asked Pete.

"Let's see how many pumpkins equal Daddy," Ricky replied.

"Well, if it doesn't break the cart," said Pam with a worried look.

"Oh, I don't think it will," said Pete. They kept putting pumpkins into the rear of the cart and, finally, Pete placed a big one on the back step.

"There it goes!" Ricky cried, as Domingo's four feet were lifted an inch off the ground.

"Ee-aw!" protested the burro.

"It's okay, Domingo," said Pete, and quickly rolled the last pumpkin back onto the ground.

Pam counted their cargo. "Daddy equals twenty-four pumpkins," she said with a laugh. "Are you satisfied, Ricky?" The answer was a wide grin as the boy started leading Domingo back toward the roadstand.

"Goodness! What a big load!" Mrs. Johnson exclaimed after the pumpkins had been laid carefully on the ground.

"We're making lots of money for Mr. Johnson," Holly remarked.

"You children have done enough for today," the woman said. "Wouldn't you like to play for a while?"

"Sue and I'd rather tend the stand," Holly declared. "We could do it alone, if you don't want to stay."

"Well, just for a little while," Mrs. Johnson agreed. "I'll get supper started."

As she walked up the drive, Pete said, "I have an idea," and beckoned to Pam and Ricky. "Why don't we poke around that little cemetery and see if we can find a clue to the treasure."

"I think it's kind of spooky," Ricky said.

"Oh, there's nothing to hurt us. Come on, now," said Pete and started back toward the secluded spot near the old barn.

Dusk was falling as the children stepped into the graveyard. How silent it was!

Pete and Pam parted the tall grass to study the old stone marker.

"I think I'd better go back now," said Ricky.

"Don't be silly!" said Pam. "There is nothing to be afraid of."

Ricky pressed behind his older brother and sister to get a better look at the carving. Suddenly

31

there came a rustling in some bushes behind them. Then, *crash!*

"Ow-ow!" Ricky cried out. "It's a spook."

Pete and Pam were startled too, and jerked around quickly enough to see Zip chasing a large rabbit through the underbrush.

After their hearts quit pounding, Pete laughed. "I wonder why we're so jumpy!" he said.

They began to giggle and Ricky, braver now, crept on hands and knees to the other side of the gravestone.

"Hey, Pete, Pam, look at this!" he said. "There's some more carving."

"Where?"

"Right here."

The other side of the marker was on the north, where the weather had worn away some of the soft stone. Still, there was enough left to identify Ricky's discovery as a circle with wings on it.

"That's odd," Pete said, getting down on his knees for a better look at the carving. "What are these little marks here, Pam? Can you make them out?"

The girl studied the circle for a moment and said, "I think that's a compass. Sure it is—look!" She made out the dim letters: N, E, S, W.

"That's right," Pete said, "the four points of the compass. But what do the wings mean?"

"The compass is flying like an angel," said Ricky and giggled.

"Do you think it could be the treasure in the

air mentioned in the verse?" Pam asked doubtfully.

Ricky snorted. "How could a compass be a treasure?"

"Crickets, I wish we could figure it out," Pete mused, as he stood on the quiet slope studying their latest clue.

But just then, their thoughts were interrupted by distant shouts.

"That's Holly," said Ricky.

"I wonder what the trouble is now," said Pam, glancing down toward the roadside stand.

Holly's screams grew higher, joined by cries from Sue.

"Come on!" Pete exclaimed. He dashed through the weeds, brushing against a milkweed pod, which sent little fluffy parachutes blowing into the air behind him. Pam and Ricky pounded at his heels.

When they reached the road, they saw what was happening. Joey and Will had arrived at the pumpkin stand on their bicycles; a metal coaster wagon was attached to the back of Joey's bike. In it was a large pumpkin. Holly was trying to wrestle it out of the wagon, while Joey and Will were endeavoring to pull her away.

"What's going on here?" cried Pete.

"That's my pumpkin!" said Joey.

"Get your hands off my sister," Ricky demanded.

"He paid for it," said Will.

"Watch out!" shouted Will.

Sue held a bill in her hands, "It's fake money! It's a counter-footer!" she cried out.

Pam quickly examined the bill. "Pete, it's stage money," she said.

"Then the pumpkin doesn't belong to you, Joey!" Pete declared. He grasped the bully by the shoulder and wheeled him about.

"Cut it out!" cried Joey. He broke loose and grabbed up the pumpkin. Pete tried to wrest it from him. Both tugged and grew red-faced. Suddenly Joey pulled the pumpkin out of Pete's arms and teetered backward toward the handsome jack-o'-lantern that Sue and Holly had helped Mrs. Johnson make.

"Watch out!" shouted Will. But it was too late. Joey sat down hard on the pumpkin and with a crunch it broke into pieces. At the same moment, Joey dropped his booty and Pete seized it. When the bully struggled up off the ground, the seat of his pants was covered with mashed pumpkin. As he furiously wiped away the yellow strings and seeds, Mrs. Johnson hastened to see what all the ruckus was about.

"Joey has pumpkin pants!" declared Sue, her eyes dancing. "Isn't that funny, Mrs. Johnson?"

CHAPTER 4

CURIE-US

FURIOUS, Joey Brill shook his fist at the Hollisters. "I'll get you for this!" he said, and hopped on his bike. But his pants were so slippery against the bicycle seat that he had to stand up to pedal down the road.

"My, what a naughty boy," Mrs. Johnson said, as Pete carried the pieces of the broken pumpkin into a field behind the roadstand. "You've done a wonderful job today," she added, "but I think it's time for you to go home now."

No sooner had she spoken than a pickup truck pulled alongside the road.

"Hi there, Indy!" Ricky called out to the sturdy-looking man who stepped out of the vehicle. Indy Roades worked for Mr. Hollister at The Trading Post. This was a combination hardware, toy, and sporting-goods store in the middle of Shoreham.

"Your dad sent me to get you," Indy said, and Sue ran up to throw herself into his arms. He was a short, ruddy-skinned man with jet-black hair and a bright smile. Indy was a real Indian and had come from New Mexico, where his tribe lived.

"But what will we do with Domingo and the cart?" Holly asked.

Indy said that Mr. Hollister had suggested that the burro live at the Johnsons' farm while the children were helping with the pumpkins.

"And Zip can stay and keep him company," said Sue.

"That's fine," the farmer's wife said. "Zip and Domingo will be good company for our goats in the new barn."

When the burro had been unhitched and led to a stall next to the goats, the children said good-by to their pets, climbed into their father's truck, and were soon delivered to their home.

After supper, Pete had just finished his homework when the doorbell sounded. Holly raced to open it, and Dave Mead stepped inside. Dave, a tall, happy-go-lucky boy, was Pete's friend. As usual, his straight hair was tousled and hung in his eyes. He lived several houses down the road.

"Hi, Dave," Pete said. "Having trouble with your homework?"

"No, mine's all finished," was the reply.

"Mine, too," said Pete with a smile.

"I want to show you something," Dave continued. "I think you'd be interested."

"A mystery?" asked Pete.

"Sort of mysterious."

With a motion of his head, Pete beckoned

Dave to his room on the second floor, where his friend sat on the edge of the bed. "I saw something in the supermarket this afternoon."

"Are they selling coaster wagons to compete with Dad's store?"

"No, nothing like that," Dave responded with a wave of his hand. "It's that new bulletin board they have."

"The one where people put up notices for things to buy and sell?"

"That's right. There's something very interesting on it—and the store's open tonight."

Pete grinned. "Okay, I'll bite. Let's go."

After Pete had asked permission of his mother to leave, he tossed on a warm jacket and went to the garage for his bike. He tested his battery-powered headlight, then pedaled off, followed by Dave on his bicycle.

While they rode side by side, Pete poured out the story of their latest mystery.

"That's keen!" Dave said. "Well, here's the supermarket."

The big store was located in a new shopping plaza near the edge of town. The two boys left their bikes in a rack, and hastened inside as the electric-eye door flew open for them.

The lads hurried through the white shiny market, dodging customers pushing carts, and soon came to the rear of the store, where a large bulletin board was fixed to the wall. On it were all kinds of notices.

Pete chuckled as he read: LITTER OF KITTENS LOOKING FOR A GOOD HOME. Another one said: A PAIR OF BOYS' ICE SKATES—WILL TRADE FOR A SMALL BICYCLE.

Dave pointed to a neatly printed card in the left-hand corner, which read: I'M LOOKING FOR AN OLD WEATHER VANE IN THE SHOREHAM AREA. IF YOU HAVE ONE, LEAVE A MESSAGE HERE. It was signed: CURIE-US.

Pete shrugged and looked at Dave. "Somebody wants an antique weather vane, I guess, but why must he be so secret about his name?"

"That's what I mean," Dave said. "Isn't that kind of mysterious?"

"I wonder if it's a lady or a man?"

"A lady," Dave guessed. "Aren't they more curious than men?"

Pete laughed. "I guess we're pretty curious to come here, and we're boys!"

"I have an old weather vane," said Dave. "It's in our attic. Do you suppose I should leave a message for Curie-Us?"

"Sure. Why not? Maybe you can make a little money by selling it."

Dave pulled a folded piece of paper from his pocket. He had already written: CONTACT DAVE MEAD, and gave his address. He took a thumbtack from a neat row of them at the top of the bulletin board and tacked his message beside that of Curie-Us.

"Crickets! I wonder what'll happen now," Pete said as they left the store.

On the way to school the next morning, the Hollisters' friends begged to hear what had happened at the farm the afternoon before.

Pam told them, and when she came to the part about Joey Brill, they all laughed.

"We'd like to help you today, if we could," Ann Hunter said.

Her eight-year-old brother, Jeff, spoke up. "Me too."

"And me," chimed in Donna Martin, who was Holly's friend. She was a plump seven-year-old with dimpled cheeks. Dave Mead also asked if he might join the Hollisters in helping Farmer Johnson.

"Yikes!" Ricky said, seeing how fast he could walk along the edge of the curbstone, "the more the merrier!"

Before they entered the school building, Dave whispered to Pete, "I wonder whether Curie-Us will answer my note today?"

Just then the bell clanged and they hurried to their classrooms.

After school, the Hollisters waited in front of their house, until their friends had arrived. Sue, remaining with her mother, waved good-by as the caravan of bicycles set off for the farm.

When they arrived, Domingo was quickly hitched to the cart and the youngsters laughed and joked as they led the burro into the pumpkin field. With all hands helping, the cart was quickly filled and soon a new stack of yellow pumpkins were piled beside the roadstand.

Mr. Johnson, busy with other farm chores, was pleased to see how well the children were working. More and more cars were stopping to buy the produce.

"My, what a big family you have," remarked one customer.

"They don't belong to me," Mrs. Johnson answered with a smile. "But I wish they did!"

Soon the children had finished the afternoon job. Domingo was unhitched and the moment he was back in the stall, Ricky waved his arms and cried, "Come on, now we can have some real fun!" He ran to the old barn with the others following, and climbed up into the front seat of the Ford car.

Oo-ga! Oo-ga, went the horn, and in the other barn Domingo brayed loudly.

Despite the dust and cobwebs, the rest of the children piled into the ancient vehicle. Jeff Hunter and Ricky began swaying back and forth. "Yikes!" Ricky cried. "We're going a hundred miles an hour!"

As he swung on the steering wheel, the left rear block slipped from under the axle and the Ford dropped backward with a jolt.

"Now you've done it!" Pete exclaimed as they all climbed out of the tilted car.

"No harm done," Pam said. "Maybe we can lift it and put the block under the axle again." But the Ford was too heavy for them to do this.

"We're going a hundred miles an hour!"

"I know how we can straighten it out," said Ricky. "We'll take the other three blocks away."

Pete agreed. Dave Mead thought this was a good idea, too. So, with all the children shoving, the car was pushed forward several inches.

Bing. Bang. Bop. The three remaining wheels hit the barn floor and the car was level again.

Pete looked it over. "Crickets! Four flat tires!"

Now Dave got behind the wheel and imagined he was driving. "Come on, old Tin Lizzie," he said. "Get going!"

Just then Mr. Johnson appeared at the barn door. "Dave? Dave Mead?" he called out.

"Uh-oh," Dave said in a low voice. "Maybe he doesn't like what we're doing." In a clear voice he said, "I'm sorry, Mr. Johnson, don't you want us to play with the car?"

"Oh, it's not that, Dave," the farmer said, smiling. "There's a man wants to see you. He's down by the stand."

Dave and Pete walked on ahead of the others to meet the man who was waiting.

The fellow was very short and stocky and appeared to be in his twenties. "Which one of you is Dave Mead?"

"I am."

"Your mother said I could find you here."

"Is there something I can do for you?" Dave asked politely.

"Maybe. I saw you answered my ad. I'm Curie-Us."

43

Pete's eyes quickly took in the details of the man's dress. He wore a gray topcoat, a blue wool suit, and pointed black shoes.

"I'd like to see the weather vane you have," the man said. "Hop in my car and I'll drive you home."

Dave exchanged a quick look with Pete, then replied, "No sir, I'd rather ride my bike home. I'll meet you there." The man nodded, strode to his car, and drove off.

After the youngsters had said good-by to the farmer and his wife, the procession of bicycles started toward home. At the Hollisters' front yard they dispersed. Ricky, Holly and Pam stayed home, but Pete and Dave rode on to the Meads' house to find Curie-Us parked in front.

"Wait here, sir, and I'll bring the weather vane," Dave said.

He and Pete went up to the attic, and rummaged around for a few minutes before finding a flat, black weather vane in the shape of a rooster. They hastened out to show it to the man. He glanced at it briefly and shook his head. "No, that's not the kind," he said. "This is a flat one. I'm looking for a three-fourths-full vane."

"Well, what is that like?" asked Dave.

"It has a fatter body to it," the man replied, "—almost fully rounded."

"Oh, yes," said Pete. "I think I know what kind you mean."

Curie-Us eyed the two boys carefully before ut-

44

tering his next words. "How would you like to work for me? I'll pay you well."

"Doing what?" asked Pete.

"Helping me to look for a special weather vane," the man replied.

"What's special about it?" Dave asked.

"It's in the form of a golden witch," Curie-Us replied.

CHAPTER 5

A TELEPHONE TIP

"A GOLDEN witch?" Dave looked perplexed. "I never saw a weather vane in the shape of a witch. Do you mean she's riding a broomstick?"

"That's right," said the stocky man. "There were all kinds of weather vanes at one time—even Indians, locomotives, and fish."

"This witch isn't solid gold, is it?" Pete asked.

"Of course not," the man replied. "It's black iron with gold leaf all over it. But that's neither here nor there. How about it? Will you boys work for me?"

Pete spoke up. "We don't even know your name."

"Never mind about that," Curie-Us replied with an impatient gesture of his hand. "I'll pay you ten dollars each if you find the right weather vane."

Dave glanced at Pete with a look of approval.

Seeing this, Curie-Us went on quickly, "Fine. Then I'll pay you in advance."

He reached for his wallet, but Pete was not in any hurry to take the money.

46

"I think I'd better ask my father about this first," Pete said.

"Don't do that," Curie-Us said curtly. "Don't say anything to anybody about this. It's a big secret."

In spite of the fact that the bills were held out to them, Pete would not take the ten dollars, and neither would Dave.

"If we find the golden-witch weather vane, that will be time enough to collect," said Pete with a grin.

"All right," Curie-Us agreed as he put his money away. "Here, take this." He wrote a phone number on a slip of paper and handed it to the blond-haired boy. "If you find the golden witch, call this number and ask for the weather-vane man."

A look of mischief came into Pete's eyes and he said, "Crickets, how many names do you have?" This remark did not please Curie-Us.

"Enough of making jokes," he said. "Find the golden witch and we'll all have a laugh then." The man returned to his car, without a backward glance, and drove off.

"What do you make of him?" Dave asked.

Pete straddled the bicycle frame and shook his head. "There's something strange going on. That must be a valuable weather vane."

Dave nodded. "We're getting into a mystery, I think."

Pete grinned as he slid onto the bicycle seat. "Between Curie-Us and the odd doings at the farm, we're going to be mighty busy." He waved and set off for home.

Pete did not tell his family about Curie-Us until they were all at the supper table. After he had finished the story, Mrs. Hollister said, "Pete, you're doing the right thing. Never keep anything like this from your parents."

"Yikes!" said Ricky. "We can all look for the golden witch. Think what we could do with ten dollars."

"Never mind the money," Pam told her brother and continued, "Officer Cal ought to know about this. Perhaps he can trace that phone number and find out who Curie-Us really is."

When her parents agreed that this would be a good idea, Pete telephoned Officer Cal Newberry at the Shoreham police headquarters. Officer Cal was a special friend of the Hollister children, and several times before had helped them in solving their mysteries. The handsome young policeman, however, insisted that it was the Hollisters who had helped *him* clear up several baffling cases.

Officer Cal promised to help, and one hour later, while the youngsters were in the dining room doing their homework, the phone rang. Pete ran to answer. After a short conversation, he hurried back.

"Guess what! The phone number belongs to the Shoreham Hotel and the fellow is registered as C. J. Yagar. He gave his address as Cleveland, Ohio."

The children and their parents talked over the

new mystery. How did Yagar know that the witch was in the Shoreham area?

"Maybe he's a collector," Pam suggested, "and has read a lot of books about special weather vanes."

"Could the golden witch have been made in Shoreham, Daddy?" Holly asked.

"Possibly," her father replied. "There were factories in town years ago, just as there are now."

"Who could tell us about them?" Ricky asked.

Pete thought of a friend of theirs who was an editor on the local newspaper. "Mr. Kent could, I bet. I'll call him tomorrow."

Next morning the youngsters were awakened by rain on the roof, so they donned raincoats and boots to go to school. On the way, Pam met Ann and told her about Curie-Us. Ann's eyes sparkled with excitement. "A golden witch! That makes it a real Halloween mystery!"

By the time the afternoon-dismissal bell rang, it was raining harder than ever, although the weather had warmed considerably.

"Crickets," Pete said, as they started home, "this is no day to sell pumpkins!"

"Let's sail boats, instead," suggested Holly. She was walking on the curb, watching the water rush along the gutter.

"It's like a river!" she exclaimed, and picked up a big twig from under a tree. "Look, Pam, this is a canoe!" As the boys walked ahead, Holly dropped the twig into the water and ran beside the bobbing stick as it rushed toward a storm sewer at the next corner. "Catch it, Pam," Holly cried. "It's going over the falls!"

Pam raced ahead and bent over to pick up the twig. As she did, her hat fell off and was swept toward the catch basin.

"Help! My hat!"

At the corner, Pete and Ricky turned to see the rain hat swirling into the opening. Pete leaped into the water and caught the brim just in time.

"Saved!" shouted Holly, running up to the boys.

"My feet are soaked," said Pete as he splashed back to the sidewalk. "Crickets, the water went right over the tops of my boots. I might as well take 'em off."

"I'm going to do that, too," declared Ricky. He started to pull off his boots.

"Me, too," said Holly. "Come on, Pam!"

"Maybe we oughtn't to," said Pam.

"Why not?" asked her sister. "It won't hurt if your feet get wet. Your head is soaking."

Pam laughed and in a few minutes all four children were running barefoot, splashing through the largest puddles.

When they reached the house, Pam and Holly were ahead of the boys, giggling.

"Then we'll do it this afternoon!" Holly said.

"Do what?" asked Ricky.

"Make invitations for our Halloween party, that's what," Holly replied.

"I want to help too," said Ricky, as the children

"Help! My hat!"

shook their raincoats in the rear vestibule before entering the kitchen.

When Mrs. Hollister saw the barefoot youngsters, she shook her head, smiling, and sent Sue upstairs for towels. In a short time the four had shoes and socks on and Pam had dried her hair. Then their mother served hot chocolate with marshmallows.

When the last drop was gone, Pam hurried to get some orange paper while Holly went to her room for a pencil. They cleared the kitchen table and began to draw pumpkins. Ricky cut them out and then Pam showed him how to make little flat hats that could be stuck into slits in the tops. If the person invited to the party could come, he was supposed to slip the hat onto the pumpkin and return it to the Hollisters.

Sue watched Pete put faces on the pumpkins while Pam made the guest list. First she put down the names of Detective Club members—Ann and Jeff Hunter, Dave Mead and Donna Martin. "Alma Brown and Mary Hancock," she said, adding two girls from school.

"And Mary's brother, Ralph," Holly reminded her.

"How about Jimmy Cox and Ned Quinn," Ricky asked with a grin. "Ned's Holly's boyfriend."

"He is not," said Holly hotly.

"How about Jimmy, then?" teased Ricky.

Holly grew red. "He'd better not pull my pigtails again or he'll be sorry."

"We'll ask them," said Pam, smiling. "Let's invite Bobby Reed, too." Bobby was a thin, ten-year-old boy whom the Hollisters had befriended while solving a mystery some time before.

The children also agreed to ask Roger Kent, the editor's son, and Don Wells, who was Pete's friend, as well as several other children from school.

Then Pam said, "What about Joey and Will?"

"Ugh, them!" said Ricky.

"Now, Ricky, be charitable," his mother said. "I don't think those boys mean to be naughty all the time."

"Only ninety-nine per cent," said Ricky.

"But, oh, let's invite them," said Pam.

"Sure, they'll make trouble either way," was Ricky's dubious reply.

After the pumpkin faces, hats, and invitations had been slipped into the envelopes and addressed, Pam said, "Now we have to get ready for the party. It's next Thursday, a week from tomorrow."

"I know something we can do for it right now," Ricky remarked.

"What?" asked Sue.

"We can practice ducking for apples."

Pete quickly got a pailful of water and carried it to a corner of the kitchen. Then he dropped three red apples into the pail and they bobbed about.

"Holly's turn first," said Ricky.

The girl tied her pigtails behind her head so they would not get wet, then bent her face toward the bobbing apples. Ricky hovered close to her. When

Holly's nose nearly touched the water, Ricky put his hand out toward her head. "Ricky!" Pam said quickly. "Stop that!"

Startled, Ricky looked about innocently. "I was only going to pat her."

"Oh, no, you weren't," Pam said sternly. Just then Holly plucked an apple from the water. She had caught the stem in her teeth and now held up the fruit triumphantly.

"Yikes!" Ricky thought to himself. "I'm going to play this trick on somebody *yet*." Aloud, he declared, "That's good Holly. Now it's my turn."

But Ricky had to duck his face all the way into the water before his teeth bit into an apple and he hauled it out. He had to run for a heavy towel to dry himself.

Pete, meanwhile, had telephoned Mr. Kent at the *Shoreham Eagle*. From him he learned that years ago there had been a company in town which had manufactured weather vanes among other things. The name was the Bennet Foundry Company.

"The foundry closed down," Mr. Kent said. "Now the building is used to manufacture paper cups."

The editor remembered a feature story that had appeared in the paper some years before about the old Bennet Foundry. He added, "The watchman for the paper-cup company used to work for the foundry. He's there in the evenings, Pete. Why don't you go down and see him?"

The rain had let up after supper, and, as it was Wednesday night, Mr. Hollister's store was open.

Pete and Pam prevailed upon their father to drop them off at the paper-cup factory before going to The Trading Post.

"Don't worry about us," Pete said as they stepped out of the station wagon. "We'll meet you later at the store."

It had already grown dark, and the only light in the factory came from a window next to the side door. The youngsters approached and Pete knocked. The door was opened by a tall, thin man. He was old, and he peered down at the children from above gold-rimmed spectacles. He even tipped his peaked cap when he saw Pam standing beside her brother.

"Are you the man who used to work at the foundry?" asked Pete.

"That's me, Josiah Applegate," said the watchman, smiling. "Won't you come in?"

The children entered a small office with a wooden table and chair in it. Pete asked if the foundry had made weather vanes.

"Oh, yes," Mr. Applegate replied. "We made many different kinds. In fact," he went on, "the iron molds of some of the vanes were left in the storeroom here."

"Crickets!" Pete declared. "Do you suppose we could see them?"

The watchman glanced at a large gold timepiece that he pulled from his pocket. "I haven't time to show 'em to you," he said, but added quickly, "you can look for yourselves. I have to start my rounds." He handed the children a key and pointed down a long, dark corridor. "It's the last room on the left side," he said. "And here, take this flashlight. You'll need it."

Pam carried the flashlight; Pete, the key. They walked silently along the corridor until they came to the right door. Pete inserted the key, but it would not turn. After the third try, the lock worked. As the door opened, Pam flashed the beam into the dark room. A smell of old iron came out, in spite of the fact that a window on the other side was half open.

"Boy! What a lot of junk!" Pete said.

Suddenly Pam grasped her brother's arm. "Look!" she exclaimed. An iron weather vane stuck up from a pile of old molds and was slowly spinning around!

CHAPTER 6

A TALL TRICK

THE weather vane spun eerily in the empty room. "Crickets," Pete said, "what's making it go round?"

"There's no breeze," Pam remarked, beaming her flashlight on the open window. "Somebody must have gone out that way and brushed against it."

Pete and Pam climbed over piles of iron molds to look out the window. A nearby street lamp cast a pool of light on the wet pavement, but no one was in sight.

"Maybe the prowler left a clue," Pete said, peering at the worn wooden window sill. There was no telltale mark. Then he stopped the slowly spinning vane, which was shaped like an arrow. "Look!" he exclaimed, and pointed to a dark fragment of cloth caught on the sharp tip. Carefully, he pulled it off.

"It's a piece of dark-blue wool," Pam observed. "You said Curie-Us wore a dark-blue suit! Do you think . . . ?"

"Yes, I do!" Pete exclaimed. "I bet it *was*

Curie-Us. After all, why would anybody else be interested in these old molds. He's looking for a clue here, the same as we are."

"But he's acting undercover," Pam added. "I wonder why."

"Let's see if the mold is here," Pete suggested. "If we find it, we'll know for sure that the Bennet Foundry Company made witches."

Lifting with all their might, Pete and his sister moved the molds and examined them. They found an eagle, a rooster, a horse and buggy, a cow, and a ship, but no witch.

"Perhaps the witch mold was broken or thrown away," Pete remarked. "If we could only find some old factory records!"

Further search of the room revealed no ledgers or books. Disappointed, Pete and Pam closed the window, left the room, and locked the door.

When the children reached the watchman's office, it was empty, so they put the key and the flashlight on the table. Then they groped toward the side door.

"Hey!" A voice startled them. "Where are you going?"

Hearts thudding, Pete and Pam whirled about to face the glare of the watchman's flashlight.

"We were going home," Pete said. "Thanks for letting us look around." Then he and Pam told about the intruder.

The watchman frowned. "The lock's been broken on that storeroom window for sometime. I've told the janitor about it, but I guess he didn't fix it."

Before Pete could ask him anything about the golden witch, Mr. Applegate excused himself and started off on his rounds again.

Once outside, Pam looked disappointed and said, "We didn't get to ask Mr. Applegate if he'd ever heard of the golden witch."

"We'll have to get in touch with him tomorrow," Pete said.

As they started down the street, Pam asked, "Do you think Curie-Us found the witch mold and took it?"

"He could have, I guess, even though it might be heavy. But I don't see how the mold could help him to find the weather vane."

"You're right," his sister replied, hurrying alongside.

On the way to The Trading Post, they stopped at the Shoreham Police Station to report to Officer Cal. Pete gave him the bit of blue wool and told him about their suspicion of Curie-Us.

"There are lots of men with blue wool suits," the officer said, "but, all the same, we'll check with the hotel manager to see if Yagar went out this evening."

Officer Cal put through the call, asked his question and listened grimly to the answer. "Gone," he said to Pete and Pam as he hung up. "Yagar checked out late this afternoon and left no forwarding address."

"Maybe he found the golden witch and went home," Pam said doubtfully. "It could be that he's just a collector, after all."

"Then why make a secret out of the whole thing?" Pete countered. "No, I think he's up to something."

Officer Cal agreed and so did their father later on when the children told him of their evening's adventure.

"But what his game is, beats me," Mr. Hollister said as he turned out the store lights. On the way home in the car, the trio discussed their two mysteries, but could not think of good explanations for Yagar's disappearance or the puzzles at the Johnson farm.

When they arrived, Mr. Hollister parked in the drive and they all went in the front door. The living room was dark, but there was a light coming from the kitchen along with the voices of Mrs. Hollister and the other three children.

Pete and Pam burst in to find them sitting around the table, playing a game.

"Hi," said Holly without looking up, "I'm winning."

As Pam was about to reply, the words froze on her lips. She grabbed Pete's arm and pointed toward the window. "Look!"

Peering in at them was a scary golden-witch face! Sue screeched and ran to her mother.

"Yikes!" exclaimed Ricky and jumped up. The face vanished.

"Look!"

"It's somebody playing a joke," declared Pete and raced out the back door, followed by Pam, Ricky, and Holly. They ran around the side of the house.

"Listen," Pete commanded. They paused in the cold, sharp air, but heard no sound of anyone running away.

Pam was first to examine the earth under the lighted kitchen window. She pointed to two square holes in the ground.

"Who do you think it was?" asked Holly, shivering.

"Somebody on stilts," Pete said.

"Three guesses," Ricky added grimly. "Good old Joey."

"Or good old Will," Pete agreed.

"They must have found out that we're looking for a golden witch," Pam said.

"Too bad Zip is at the farm," Holly put in. "He might have caught the spook."

Next morning the Hollisters divided the invitations and delivered them to their friends in school. Pam told Ann about the witch scare the night before, but the first bell rang before her chum could say anything.

That afternoon Pam and Ann walked home together and talked over plans for the party. "The invitations are darling," Ann said. "I'm coming, of course, and so is Jeff." Then she told Pam that her father knew a candy manufacturer. "I can bring boxes of licorice cats and those little creamy orange pumpkins."

"That would be wonderful," Pam said.

As the two girls approached the Hunters' house, Pam saw Joey Brill disappear around the corner of the porch.

"Now what's he up to, I wonder," she said.

The girls ran over to the porch, but Joey had raced off. Pam glanced down. "Look at this, Ann!" she exclaimed. There were stilt marks beside the house! "They're all over your front yard," Pam said as she followed the tracks. "Joey Brill paid you a visit last night, too."

Ann looked down at the holes. "They certainly do look like stilt tracks," she remarked.

"I have to go," Pam said. "Mother's waiting." Promising to see her friend next day, Pam hurried home, where she found Mrs. Hollister at the wheel of the station wagon, ready to take the children to the Johnsons' farm.

When they arrived, the farmer met them with a grin and promised a return ride in his truck. As the young helpers piled out in front of the farmhouse, Ricky and Holly volunteered to tend the roadstand.

"All right," agreed Mr. Johnson. "Then Pete and Pam can take a load of apples to the mill, in the cart."

"Oh, I want to ride in the apple cart, too," piped Sue.

"I'm afraid you might upset it, darling," said Mrs. Hollister with a twinkle.

"Let her stay, Mother," Pam begged. "We'll watch her."

"All right, dear," Mrs. Hollister said, and drove off. Ricky and Holly raced to the roadstand as the other three followed Mr. Johnson to the barn. Pete and Pam harnessed Domingo while the farmer lifted five bushel baskets of apples into the wagon. Pam boosted Sue in, climbed in beside her, and took the reins.

"Should we bring the cider back?" Pam asked.

The farmer smiled. "No. I don't think Aunt Nettie'll be able to put these apples through today." He explained that some mills took the apples and immediately gave the customer jugs of cider made from other apples. "But I want the juice from my own fruit," he said. "These are dandies—some are tart, some sweet. It takes all kinds to make good cider. Taste 'em," he invited, and tossed each of the children a shiny apple.

As Pete bit into the bright-red skin, Mr. Johnson pointed to a narrow opening among the trees.

"That's the old cart road," he said. "You follow it straight up the hill and down the other side. The mill's at the bottom; you can't miss it."

"Are there bears in the woods?" asked Sue.

The farmer chuckled. "No. Nothing but deer and a few little wild critters."

Pete clucked his tongue at Domingo, and the burro started off with the boy walking alongside.

The cart entered the woods and in a few moments passed by the old barn. The sagging building loomed up behind the trees and seemed to lean toward the children. There was no sound but the creak of wagon wheels and the crunch of sticks under Domingo's feet.

When the way became steeper, Pete helped the burro by pushing the back of the cart up the rutted road to the top of the hill. They stopped on the ridge.

"Hush," Pam said. "I heard a deer or something."

Sue put her finger to her lips and sat silent. A crow cawed from the top of a distant tree.

"We'd better go on now," Pete said. Suddenly there was a rustling noise in the woods behind them.

"Listen!" said Pam, and Pete halted the burro.

"Somebody's walking in the leaves," Pete declared.

The rustling sound came closer.

"Who's there?" Pete called.

The noise stopped. There was no reply.

CHAPTER 7

SLINGSHOT FLAGPOLE

PAM's heart skipped wildly and she exchanged worried looks with Pete. Who could be following them through the woods?

As suddenly as the footsteps had stopped, they began again! Pam put an arm around Sue and drew her little sister close as a patch of red appeared from among the trees.

All at once, a young woman in a scarlet jacket stepped into the lane beside them. "Well, this is a surprise!" she said. "I didn't expect to see a donkey cart!"

"Crickets! We're surprised, too," Pete said with a big sigh. He noticed that she was short and had dark hair like the young woman he and Pam had seen prowling around the Johnson farm!

"We called 'Who's there?'" Pam said. "Didn't you hear us?"

"I wasn't sure," the stranger replied, "so I stopped to listen." As she spoke, she came abreast of Domingo. On the back of her jacket the children saw a yellow deer head and under it the words: BUNTING DEER FARM.

"What a darling burro," the young woman said, and stroked the little animal's ears. "I see you're headed for the cider mill. I'm going that way, too."

Pete stood stiffly beside Domingo, his eyes on the telltale jacket. The young woman saw his look. Then she glanced up at Pam in the cart and noticed that she, too, had a doubtful expression.

"Is something wrong?"

"Well," said Pete, "we've seen you before."

"You have? Where?"

"Coming out of Farmer Johnson's old barn last Sunday."

"And in the little graveyard," Pam added. "We called to you and you ran away."

The woman studied the children's serious faces, then chuckled. "Don't look at me like that," she said. "I haven't done anything wrong."

"You sure acted suspicious," Pete retorted.

"I would have answered you," came the reply, "but just at that moment I spotted Ambrose in the woods and had to run after him."

"Who's Amber nose?" asked Sue. They all smiled, and the woman went on.

"He's my deer." She stuck her hands up on each side of her head, like horns. Now all three children laughed.

"You see, I own a deer farm across the road from the cider mill. Ambrose is my special pet, but he likes to run away. I was searching for him Sunday."

"Did you find him?" asked Sue.

67

"Yes," was the reply, "but he got away this afternoon and here I am, on the trail again!"

"We'll help you look," said Pete and led Domingo forward.

As the cart rolled downhill, the children introduced themselves to the young woman, who said that her name was Katherine Bunting.

Hearing this, Sue rolled her eyes. "Where are your long ears and pink nose, Miss Bunny?"

Katherine Bunting laughed. "That's a cute nickname. Why don't you all call me Bunny?"

"All right, Bunny," said Pam, greatly relieved by the young woman's friendly manner.

On the way to the cider mill, she told them about her deer farm. "We get many visitors who come to feed and pet the animals. I really need a larger place."

"Maybe you ought to see Mr. Johnson," Pete suggested. "He was talking about selling part of his farm."

"Was he now?" said Bunny, widening her big eyes. "Thanks for telling me. I'll phone him."

Bunny explained that if she had more room she would put in an animal nursery. "I'd have baby ducks, and chicks as well as kids and lambs. Then I'd sell bottles of milk so that children could feed the animal babies."

Sue clapped her hands. "And we could pet the soft woolly lambs!"

Finally the road leveled off and they came out into a clearing. To one side was a low red wooden building and behind it an open shed with bushels of apples in it. Nearby stood a Jeep.

"This is where I leave you," Bunny said. She pointed to a road that led past the mill. "My deer farm is just a skip and a jump down the road to the right. Come see me when you can."

"Wait," said Pam, "before you go!" Quietly she asked if Bunny had honked the horn of the ancient automobile the day she had looked in the old barn for the deer.

"No," Bunny replied. "I didn't. Why do you ask?"

Confident of their new friend, Pam told her of the treasure mystery.

"Sorry I can't help you," Bunny said kindly. Then she kissed Sue on the cheek and hurried off. As she passed the mill, Bunny knocked on the door. "Nettie," she called, "come out! You have customers."

A moment later the door opened and out came a tall, square-built woman wearing a yellow apron. She walked over to the cart as Pam scrambled to the ground.

"I know you," Aunt Nettie said in a forceful voice. "Mr. Johnson called to say you were coming." She adjusted her glasses, reached up her brawny arms, and swung Sue off the cart.

"You're the Hotsoler children, aren't you?" the mill woman said as she began unloading bushels of apples from the cart.

"Hollister," the three chorused.

"I never heard the name before," said Aunt Nettie. "I've been living around here a good many years. I thought I knew about everybody. But I don't know Hotsolers."

Sue opened her mouth, but Pam signaled her to be quiet. She and Pete managed to swallow their smiles.

Suddenly Pete got an idea. "If you've lived here a long time," he said, "maybe you've heard of a golden-witch weather vane."

"Weather vane?" Aunt Nettie asked in surprise. "Golden witch! Can't say I have. But wait. There *is* a gold weather vane on the flagpole down at the old schoolhouse."

"Is it a witch?" Pam asked excitedly.

Aunt Nettie shrugged. "I don't know," she replied. "I never did see any good at a distance and I can't say I ever took much notice."

"Where's the school?" Pam asked.

"'Bout half mile down the road," the woman replied, pointing to the left.

Quickly Pete and Pam decided to go look at the weather vane. Sue wanted to see inside the mill, so Aunt Nettie agreed to care for her until they returned.

Pete and Pam trotted down the road, passing only a few houses. Finally they came to a small white frame building set in a field of weeds and crowned with a wooden cupola. Over the door was a weather-beaten sign: CLARETON TOWNSHIP SCHOOL.

"This must be it," Pam said. "Where's the flag-pole?"

"Over there, behind the bushes near the back of the school."

The brother and sister pushed through the weeds until they came to the base of the pole, made of steel pipe.

Pete and Pam peered up at the top. They could see a glitter of gold but could not make out what the figure was.

"If that's a witch, it sure is a funny one," said Pete. "I'll have to climb up there for a better look."

"Well," said Pam doubtfully, "be careful. That pole doesn't look very strong to me."

Pete began to shin up the staff. Pam held onto it, but could not stop it from swaying.

Suddenly, as Pete neared the top, the pole bent sharply toward the school building.

"It's going to break!" Pam screamed.

Pete let go and flung himself toward the school roof. As he landed on the shingles, the flagpole *swooshed* back and the gold object on the top flew off like a stone from a slingshot.

Pam raced to the side of the schoolhouse. "Are you all right?" she called up to Pete.

"I'm okay," her brother replied, "but the weather vane is gone." Shading his eyes from the setting sun, he looked around, then pointed to a spot in the tall grass. "I see something gold over there."

With Pete calling "warm" and "cold," Pam searched until her hand touched a piece of metal.

71

"It's going to break!"

"It's a gold eagle," the girl called out, "but it isn't a weather vane at all—just an ornament."

Disappointed, Pete climbed down a rickety drainspout and jumped to the ground. "Crickets," he said as Pam handed him the eagle. "It hasn't even got a head. What'll we do with it now?"

"We can't put it back." She suggested that they take the ornament to the Clareton Town Hall on Saturday.

Pete agreed and they trudged toward the cider mill. When they arrived it was the hazy time between night and day and the air had the fresh smell of damp falling leaves.

"I love the autumn," Pam said, taking a deep breath. Suddenly she noticed the absence of Domingo and the cart, and just as quickly heard her little sister's pleading voice coming from behind the apple shed.

"Domingo! Don't eat so much!"

Pete and Pam hurried around the corner of the shed. There was Domingo, still attached to the cart, with his nose deep in a pile of what looked like chunks of newspapers soaked in the rain. Sue was trying to pull him away, but the burro kept eating.

"Crickets! What's that stuff?" Pete exclaimed. Just then Aunt Nettie came up behind them. "It's pomace," she said. "That's what's left of the apples after they've been pressed for cider. All the wild animals love it—especially deer."

73

"We're sorry Domingo ate so much," Pam apologized.

"Bless you," said Aunt Nettie, "I have oodles of it—enough for you to take home for Domingo's dinner all week long."

With Pete helping, she shoveled two bushel baskets full. After thanking her, the children climbed into the cart. Pete took the reins and they started up the road through the woods.

It was nearly dark when they finally glimpsed the dilapidated barn through the trees. In spite of himself, Pete shivered and urged Domingo to go faster. Then, drawing nearer, Pam seized her brother's arm.

"Listen!"

Pete halted the cart. At that moment the barn door slowly creaked open.

The old Ford was inching out, but there was nobody in the driver's seat!

CHAPTER 8

A BIG TUMBLE

PETE, Pam, and Sue stared in amazement when the back end of the car came into view. Ricky and Holly were pushing it!

Pete jumped down from the cart and ran to his brother. "What do you two think you're doing?" he demanded sternly.

"Oh, hi," said Ricky. "We want to get a better look at the old jalopy. Holly figured out how to release the brake."

"You scared us," Pam said, laughing. "I guess we all have the Halloween jitters," she added. "We'd better push the car back. It's too dark to see it now."

"We'll all help," Sue offered, and held open the sagging barn door as the four older children pushed the automobile back inside. As soon as the door was closed again, they hastened to the new barn, where a light shone from a window.

Zip came bounding out past Farmer Johnson's truck to greet them.

While the excited collie barked and licked the

children, Pam and Ricky unloaded the baskets of pomace outside the barn door.

"If we take it inside," Pete reasoned, "Domingo and the goats might get at it and eat too much."

Once Domingo was unhitched, the youngsters went inside to help the farmer give fresh grain and water to the animals. Pete told about the headless eagle and Mr. Johnson said they could leave it in the barn. "No great damage done," he added. "Saturday is time enough to take it back."

"Not to change the subject," said Ricky, rubbing his nose with the back of his hand, "but that Tin Lizzie's a great old car, Mr. Johnson. Do you think it'll run?"

The man smiled and tousled Ricky's red hair. "Might be some life in the old girl, yet," he said. "Come on. Jump in my truck and I'll take you home."

On the way, Ricky kept thinking of the antique car. "Too bad it has to be stuck in that barn where nobody can see it," he said to himself, and his eyes narrowed with an idea.

Home again, the Hollisters found their mother arranging a row of pumpkin invitations on the living-room table.

"Nearly everyone is coming," she said, as they skimmed off their wraps.

"Who isn't?" asked Pam.

"Joey and Will."

"Hurray," Ricky said under his breath.

"They'll be sorry," announced Holly, "'cause it's

76

going to be a wonderful, scrumptious party. Maybe Daddy'll give us favors and decorations from The Trading Post. Will you, Daddy, please?"

Mr. Hollister put down the paper he was reading. "Yes. I'd be glad to."

"Yikes!" Ricky exclaimed. "What kind of favors will you give us, Dad!"

"I don't know yet. Some sort of surprise."

"And here's another surprise," their mother said. "Mrs. Johnson would like Pete, Pam, Ricky, and Holly to spend the weekend at the farm—from Friday night until Sunday."

"Me, too?" piped up Sue.

"Not this time, dear. I need somebody to help me with important things."

"Like making pies?"

"Yes," Mrs. Hollister replied with a wink at Pam. "And making costumes, too."

"Oh goody," said Sue, and hugged her mother.

Dinner time was taken up with excited chatter about the coming weekend adventure. When the last speck of dessert was finished, Pam reminded Pete to call Josiah Applegate.

Quickly the boy looked up the number of the paper-cup company and dialed it. A young-sounding man answered and told him that the watchman was not there.

"I'm his substitute," the man explained. "Mr. Applegate had some time off coming to him, and he won't be back for at least five days."

"Do you know where we could reach him?" Pete asked anxiously.

"'Fraid not," was the reply. "He's out of town."

"Maybe his family could tell us," Pete said.

"He lives alone," replied the speaker.

Disappointed, Pete thanked the man and the receiver clicked. He reported the conversation to the others.

"Well, that's a dead end," said Ricky. "Now what?"

"We'll have to find another lead," said Pam.

Then Pete telephoned Dave. The boys agreed to meet at the farm on Saturday and take the eagle to Clareton on their bicycles. "Maybe we can find a lead to the witch there," said Pete.

An hour later four bags were packed with clothing, toothbrushes, a flashlight, and other necessities.

"Now all we have to do is pick them up tomorrow afternoon," Pam said. The next day, she thought, was the longest school day of the year. Once, when she was looking out the window, her teacher caught her with a surprise question.

"I'm sorry," Pam said, blushing, "but my mind was at the pumpkin farm."

Everybody laughed, even the teacher, who repeated the question. Pam answered in a flash and got it right.

Finally the bell rang. As the Hollisters hastened home, Holly told Jeff Hunter that her father was going to give favors to everyone at the party.

"What kind?" asked Jeff.

"I don't know," said Holly. "Something nice."

Jeff's eyes sparkled. "Your father has lots of Scout knives in his store window. Do you think it'll be those?"

Holly shrugged. "Wait and see." Just then she saw Indy drive up with Mr. Hollister's truck and she raced on ahead to greet him. The bags and Pete's bike were quickly loaded and off they went.

"Hello, hello!" Mrs. Johnson called as the young visitors trooped into the farmhouse. "You don't have to gather pumpkins today. We have plenty for the stand. Run along and have a good time. I'll whistle when supper's ready."

Pete's eyes sparkled. "What luck, Pam! Let's explore the old barn. "Maybe we can find a clue to the person who honked the horn."

"Or even to Adam Cornwall's treasure."

"Yikes!" cried Ricky, and the four raced across the farmyard and up the slope among the saplings. They all stopped at the barn door to listen.

"Anyone in there?" Ricky called out.

Pam giggled nervously, and Pete swung open the sagging door. Inside, it seemed gloomier than ever. Around the dirt floor were scattered old apple crates, a rake, and some broken tools. Against one wall stood several large oil drums and above them hung a tangle of rotting harnesses.

"Look at this!" Pam walked over to a small rusty tractor and swung herself into the seat.

"Me next," Ricky begged, just as a loud booming noise filled the barn.

Holly was beating a large empty oil can like a drum. Ricky ran to join her and the banging grew like thunder.

"Please!" Pam cried.

"We're detectives—remember?" Pete said. "Quit fooling around."

"Okay, chief," Ricky said importantly.

As they searched more quietly, Pam paced from one side of the old building to the other, keeping her eyes on the blackened beams above. "Maybe the treasure is hanging from the ceiling or hidden behind a beam," she thought. "After all, that's in the air."

Holly, meanwhile, poked around the stalls. The roof had caved in across the middle of the barn and light shone into the places where the animals had been kept. On the floor lay moldy hay and rotting grain. An iron bar was sticking up from one of the narrow spaces between the wall of the stall and the side of the barn.

"I wonder what that is?" Holly thought. She was reaching for it, when Ricky shouted.

"Help, Holly, help!" She raced from the stall to see Ricky running behind a big iron wagon wheel that was rolling crazily over the uneven floor. "I've got it going," he called, "don't let it fall!"

As Holly ran beside him, helping to steer the wheel, it suddenly hit a post and dropped sideways. The two children jumped back just in time and the heavy wheel landed an inch from their toes.

"Whew!" Ricky exclaimed. As they raised the wheel again, Holly noticed that Pam was still walking slowly with her eyes on the ceiling. Right in her path lay a rake!

"Look out!" Holly cried.

Too late! Pam's foot came down on the tines and the long handle flew up and struck her on the forehead.

"Ow!" cried Pam and caught her breath. The others ran to help her.

"Are you okay?" asked Pete.

Pam held her head and felt a little bump rise.

"Gleeps! Being a detective is dangerous," Holly declared. "What were you looking at, Pam?"

Her sister pointed to a wooden ladder that led up to a loft. Below the platform lay a big pile of hay that had fallen through the broken floor.

"Maybe that's where the treasure is," Pam said, still holding her bump with one hand.

"The ladder looks pretty rickety," Pete observed.

"I'm littler than you," said Holly. "I'll go up."

"Be careful. I'll stand down here to catch you."

Holly stepped to the ladder and gingerly made her way into the loft, where she disappeared.

Silence. Then, "Pam! Come up, quick! Oh, look at this! Look at . . ."

As she spoke there was a cracking noise and then a yell as Holly came tumbling down through the loft floor. Pete dived to catch her but missed, and

Holly landed in the pile of hay below. More old hay cascaded over her head.

"I'm all right," she said, brushing straws away from her face. "But there's a big bundle up there, wrapped in brown paper."

"Crickets, maybe it's a clue to the treasure," said Pete. He ran for the ladder, advanced one rung—and *crash*.

The ladder fell apart. At the same instant came a faraway whistle.

"That's supper," said Pam. "We've got to go."

The four detectives hesitated, not wanting to leave the possible clue that Holly had found. Nonetheless, they hurried back to the farmhouse, where Pete told the Johnsons what they had discovered.

The farmer laughed. "You're determined to find that treasure, aren't you?" he said. "Well, that's fine, but you'll have to let it go for tonight. There's no light out in that barn and I don't want any more accidents."

Before they sat down to eat, Mrs. Johnson applied an ice pack to Pam's bump and it quickly grew smaller. Later, pumpkin pie with whipped cream made her forget all about it.

At bedtime the farmer's wife showed the girls to a big cheerful room on the second floor. Adjoining it was the boys' room, with a large dormer window looking out toward the woods.

Pete opened the window, looked longingly at the old barn, climbed into bed, and soon was fast asleep.

Holly came tumbling down!

In the middle of the night he was awakened by Zip barking.

Ricky sat up. "What's the matter?" he whispered.

Pete took his flashlight, hurried to the window, and beamed it toward the new barn. At the corner of the building, two green eyes glowed in the light!

CHAPTER 9

SUSPICIOUS CHARACTERS

Suddenly there was a knock at the door and Pam and Holly entered. Their faces were wide awake.

"Did you see it?" Pam whispered.

"It's a tiger or a mountain lion!" said Holly.

"Whatever it is, we'll find out," Pete declared, pulling on his robe. The others did likewise, and Pete led the single file quietly downstairs and out into the chilly starlit night.

Ricky's teeth chattered from the cold and excitement. "Maybe it's a bear or a wolf after Domingo and the goats," he said.

"Wait!" Pete ordered quietly.

Against the darkness of the barn, they could see a darker shape. The blond-haired boy flicked on his flash again.

A small deer stood in the circle of light.

"A fawn!" gasped Pam!

"And eating our pomace!" Holly said.

"Sh-sh!"

The children walked slowly toward the feeding animal. The deer turned his head to look warily into the light and seemed about to run, then bent again to the pile of apple pressings.

Pam stepped ahead of Pete and laid a hand quickly but gently on the deer's neck. Around it was a light chain collar and a tag which read: AMBROSE. BUNTING DEER FARM.

"You're a naughty deer," Pam cooed. "You'll have to spend the night here in the barn, so you don't run away from Bunny again."

She pulled the fawn away from the pomace and led him into the barn. Zip barked loudly and leaped toward them while Domingo brayed and the goats bleated.

Pete calmed the dog and Holly quieted the burro.

"Ricky, get some pomace," Pam said. "We'll give them all a midnight snack."

The redhead hurried out and returned with a basket of squeezed apples. As they fed handfuls of the pomace to the burro and deer, Pete and Pam held the three animals close to each other, so they could become acquainted. Soon the deer and the burro were eating peacefully out of the same basket and Zip gobbled a cookie Holly found in her bathrobe pocket.

In a little while, Pam put Ambrose in the stall with Domingo, and Zip lay down in front of it.

The Hollisters left the barn and hustled into the farmhouse.

86

"Yikes, I could do with a midnight snack myself," said Ricky.

"So could I," came a deep voice in the kitchen, and the light went on. There stood Mr. Johnson in the doorway, dressed in a red-plaid bathrobe.

"I was just about to come see what was keeping you," he said as he opened the refrigerator. He took out the remains of a pumpkin pie, and a bottle of milk. "I heard Domingo making a rumpus, so I looked out and saw it was only a deer."

"How could you tell?" asked Ricky.

"I know 'em well," the man replied. "They come around a lot. Then I heard the stairs creak and I saw you four going toward the barn."

After eating the sweet, spicy pie, the Hollisters thanked Mr. Johnson and returned to bed.

At breakfast Saturday morning, Pete told the farmer that Dave was coming over and that the two boys would help him.

"Good," came the reply. "We can work in the orchard."

"But what about the package in the hayloft?" Holly asked.

The farmer frowned. "I don't want you climbing there. It isn't safe. I'll help you get it down tomorrow. Besides, you have to return Ambrose."

Although impatient to see what was inside the bundle, the Hollisters agreed to wait.

As Pam, Holly, and Ricky left the farm, Zip bounded beside them. Pam held Ambrose on a clothesline leash and they made their way through the woods. The deer walked demurely, lifting his tiny feet daintily.

When the little procession passed the cider mill, Aunt Nettie waved from the doorway.

A short distance farther on, the Hollisters came to a small brown-shingled house set back from the road. At one side was a fenced-in area with open sheds, near which stood several white-faced deer.

"Oh, aren't you beautiful!" Holly cried to the deer, and ran over to put her hand through the wire fencing. The deer approached, their heads bobbing with each step.

Just then, Bunny came from behind the house, carrying a bucket. "So you found my truant," she exclaimed. "Ambrose, you're just in time for breakfast!" Bunny petted the deer, all the while leading him into the enclosure while Holly chattered about their midnight discovery.

"He pushes up the fence and squeezes under," Bunny explained. "When I get a larger place, he'll have plenty of room to roam and won't want to run away."

"I hope you get it soon," Pam said.

"If I do, I'll have you to thank," Bunny replied. "I'm going to see Mr. Johnson tonight about buying some of his land."

"Goodie! We'll be there, too," Holly said gleefully. "'By, Bunny."

At the cider mill, the youngsters stopped to see

Aunt Nettie. For a while they watched her feeding apples into the big press. Then Ricky strolled about the room and looked into a large barrel.

"Yikes," he exclaimed above the grinding sound of the press, "millions of corks!"

Aunt Nettie nodded without taking her eyes off the tumbling stream of apples. "For the bottles," she said.

"They make great floats for fishing lines," Ricky commented.

"Want some?" Aunt Nettie asked. "Help yourself. I've got oodles."

"Thanks," said Ricky happily. "Yikes, thanks," and filled all of his pockets.

In a little while the children said good-by to the busy woman and walked back to the farm. When they reached the barn, Pete and Dave were just leaving on their bicycles. In Pete's basket was a large brown-paper sack with a golden wing sticking out of it.

The two boys pedaled hard and soon their faces were glowing. When they reached Clareton, they rode to the town square.

In the center was a statue of a soldier and, behind it, an old-fashioned stone building with the words CLARETON TOWN HALL on the front. The two boys leaned their bicycles against the building. Pete took the bag from his basket and led the way up the wide front steps.

In the main hall they saw a thin, middle-aged

man with horn-rimmed glasses sitting at a reception desk.

As they approached him, Dave whispered, "Don't forget to ask if they ever heard of the witch."

The man looked up sharply over his glasses. "What was that you said?"

"Excuse me," said Pete. "We'd like to have some information."

"What kind?" he asked, and before they could speak, he added, "What have you got there?"

Pete took the headless eagle from the bag.

"Where did you get that?"

"From the flagpole at the old school. We can explain—"

"Put it on the desk and sit down over there," the man ordered, and pointed to a bench near a marble column.

As Pete and Dave obeyed, he picked up the phone and talked quietly into it, never taking his eyes off the boys.

"I don't like the way he's looking at us," Pete whispered.

"Neither do I," said Dave. They fidgeted a few minutes until a large policeman came hurrying down the hall. The receptionist rose and pointed to the boys. "There they are!" he said. "They must be the ones."

As Pete and Dave stood up, bewildered, the policeman said, "You'll have to come with me, boys."

"There they are!"

"But we haven't done anything wrong," Pete declared.

"You'll have to answer some questions," said the officer. "How'd you get that eagle?"

Quickly Pete introduced himself and Dave, then explained about searching for the golden witch. "If you don't believe us, you could call our fathers or Mr. Johnson, or Officer Cal Newberry of the Shoreham Police," Pete added.

The bespectacled man hurried back to his telephone. While he made a call, the policeman eyed the two boys steadily. Pete and Dave felt hot and uncomfortable.

In a few minutes the receptionist bustled back. "They're all right," he said. "Officer Newberry vouches for the Hollister boy."

Pete and Dave grinned in relief.

"If you don't mind telling us," said Pete, "what did you think we had done?"

The policeman smiled. "Last night, a black iron weather vane shaped like a witch disappeared from the roof of an empty house on Doyster Street. It was sawed right off."

The thin man spoke up. "When I heard you whispering about a witch and saw you with that eagle, I felt it necessary to have you questioned."

"But crickets," said Pete politely, "if we'd stolen the eagle, we wouldn't walk into the Town Hall to give it back."

"And if we'd stolen the witch," Dave went on, "we wouldn't come here to ask about witches."

"Nonetheless," said the man, "I felt you were suspicious characters. Sorry," he added stiffly.

Pete then asked if the men had ever heard of a golden-witch weather vane, but neither could offer any help.

As the boys left the building, their faces split into wide grins. "Dave, I always knew you were a suspicious character," said Pete. Then he grew serious. "Crickets! That stolen witch might be the golden one painted black!"

"And probably Curie-Us is the thief," agreed Dave.

As they mounted their bicycles, Pete shook his head. "This is a crazy mystery. If Yagar stole that witch, and it was the right one, the case is over! We'll probably never see Yagar again or find out what it was all about!"

Disappointed, the boys pedaled back to the farm and spent the afternoon working in the pumpkin field. At four o'clock, Dave mounted his bicycle and headed home.

It was dark after supper when the Hollisters went out to the barn to feed Domingo, the goats, and Zip. As the children started back to the house, the moon came out from behind the clouds. Pete glanced up the slope toward the little cemetery.

He stopped short. "Wait! I saw something move up there."

"Yikes!" muttered Ricky, but he followed the others as they crept quietly out of sight through the long grass until they were near the graveyard.

Suddenly, the weeds near the tombstone rustled. A figure rose up, then ducked down again.

Two silent words formed on Pete's lips, "Joey Brill!"

CHAPTER 10

NIGHT NOISES

Lying flat, the Hollisters peeked through the grass and waited. Joey showed his head again, and next to him appeared Will Wilson. They started to whisper.

"When do you think they'll come?" asked Will.

"Any minute now, I guess. We'll scare those Hollisters!"

"How do you know they'll pass this way?" asked Will.

"I told you," said Joey impatiently. "Ricky said they'd go to the barn after supper in the dark to feed the animals. He was bragging how they went near this place without getting scared."

Pete, Pam, and Holly turned silently to look at Ricky. His face was beet-red.

"I bet they won't show up at all," Will went on. "Let's go."

"What's the matter? You scared?"

"Course not!" replied Will, in a cracky voice.

Quickly Pete put his lips to Pam's ear and whispered a plan. "Pass it on."

Moments later, the four Hollisters circled cautiously through the high grass behind Joey and Will. Pete wriggled partway out of his jacket, then scrambled behind Adam Cornwall's tombstone.

"What was that?" whispered Will. "I heard something."

"Don't be silly," said Joey.

Holly moaned.

Will seized Joey's arm and both boys looked around wild-eyed.

"I heard something that time for sure," gasped Will. "Behind us."

Pam gave a weird howl and Ricky groaned. As the startled bullies whirled, a headless thing with two long flapping arms rose up in the moonlight from behind the tombstone.

With yells of fright, Joey and Will dashed off. Joey tripped over the railing and fell flat. Will leaped three feet over it and never looked back.

Crying for his pal to wait, Joey scrambled up and raced off into the darkness.

The Hollisters stood up, laughing.

"Oh!" Holly gasped, "wasn't it wonderful!"

"I nearly choked trying not to laugh," Pam declared.

Pete pulled his jacket off his head and slipped his arms in the sleeves. "It was great," he said. "Old Joey was really scared."

Glowing with success, the Hollisters turned their heads into the sharp wind and hurried toward the farmhouse. They arrived to find a small yellow sports car in the yard.

Joey and Will dashed off.

"Yikes! That's keen," Ricky said. "I'd like to know the fellow who owns it."

In the kitchen they found Bunny seated at the table with Mr. Johnson looking at a map of the farm.

"Is that your car?" Pam asked.

When Bunny said it was, Ricky declared admiringly, "You're swell—for a girl."

"Come, come now," said Mrs. Johnson teasingly. She was watching a big bubbling pot. "What would you do without girls? Pam, Holly, help me make doughnuts."

The farmer's wife gave the Hollister girls aprons to wear. Then she placed a big sheet of clean brown paper on a long table beside the stove. To Holly she gave a metal can with holes in the top.

"You're in charge of sugaring the doughnuts," Mrs. Johnson said. Holly grasped the can by the handle and stood ready.

Pam was sent to a smaller table on the other side of the stove. Here was a large tray heaped with doughballs and a wire basket about as large as the pot.

"Put about eight balls in the basket," the farmer's wife instructed. Pam did so, and Mrs. Johnson lowered the basket into the hot bubbling fat in the big pot.

When the doughnuts were crispy brown, she pulled out the basket and dumped them onto the brown paper in front of Holly. Nine batches were made.

When the last doughnut had been sprinkled with powdered sugar, all three cooks were pink with heat and Holly's nose was frosted white.

"Six dozen," she announced. "I counted 'em."

"When are we going to eat some?" Ricky asked.

"As soon as they're cooler," Mrs. Johnson promised.

"We'll have a doughnut feast to celebrate," Mr. Johnson spoke up. "Amy," he said to his wife, "I have just agreed to sell Miss Bunting the pasture by the road."

"I'm so pleased!" Bunny exclaimed. "I can build a little house there and have room for more animals."

"That's fine," said Mrs. Johnson. "It'll be nice to have you for a neighbor."

Bunny beamed. "Grandfather will be delighted. He can come and live with me now and help with the deer farm. He doesn't like the factory any more," she added, "since it stopped being an iron-works."

The Hollisters pricked up their ears. "Where does your grandfather work?" Pete asked.

"At the paper-cup factory in Shoreham. His name is Josiah Applegate."

"We know him!" chorused Pete and Pam. Quickly they explained about meeting the watch-man in their search for the golden witch.

Bunny grinned. "The good old golden witch!"

"You know about it?" Pete asked, excited.

Bunny laughed. "I've known about it all my life!"

As the children's questions tumbled out, she held up her hand. "Take it easy! I'll tell you my story. Years ago, Grandfather worked at the iron foundry. He used to tell my cousins and me about a special golden-witch weather vane. The person who ordered it had arranged for a very valuable object to be hidden inside it. The vanes are hollow, you know."

"What was the thing?" Holly asked.

"No one at the factory knew," was the reply. "When the time came to put in the treasure and solder the two halves of the iron witch together, a workman did the job in secret."

"Who was the workman?" Pete asked.

"I never knew his name," Bunny said, "but I remember Grandfather telling us that he had died."

"Who ordered the witch?" was Pam's next query. "That's the most important question."

"Sorry, I don't know that, either," Bunny replied.

"No wonder Yagar wanted to find that weather vane," declared Ricky. "He must know about the treasure."

"Maybe he has it by now," said Pete grimly. "If the black witch that was stolen in Clareton is the right one, we might as well forget the whole thing."

"But since we don't know," Pam said hopefully, "we'll just have to keep on searching."

"We haven't any clues," protested Ricky. "Do

you think the doughnuts are cool enough yet, Mrs. Johnson?"

"Some are," she replied. In a few minutes the woman placed a heaping platter of doughnuts on the table, while Pam brought brimming glasses of cold milk.

Ricky took a big bite into a warm, crusty doughnut. "Oh, yum!"

Suddenly Bunny stopped eating her doughnut and rolled her eyes. "I forgot!" she exclaimed. "Maybe I do have a clue for you—the foundry records!"

"Please tell us!" cried Pete.

Bunny went on, "When the Bennet Company closed, Grandfather found a box of old records the bookkeeper had left behind. He wrote to the Bennet heirs, but they told him to throw it away. Well, Grandfather can't bear to throw anything away, so he kept the box. It's in my attic now."

Pete and Pam were on their feet and ready to travel! "May we go look at them?" Pam asked.

"It's too late tonight," Mrs. Johnson put in kindly. "Tomorrow, perhaps."

"I won't be home till after supper tomorrow," Bunny said, "but I'll expect you then."

"We'll be there!" Pete promised.

"Good! I hope I bring you as much luck as you brought me," Bunny said with a smile.

Everyone went out on the porch with Bunny and watched her climb into her little car. The engine roared, she waved and moments later was gone.

As they all turned to go inside, Ricky said, "Listen!" From the barn came the noise of the goats bleating.

"Something disturbed them, I guess," said Mrs. Johnson. "Come along, it's cold out here."

When they were once more in the kitchen, Holly helped herself to another doughnut and sat thinking. Here she was in a nice warm kitchen with goodies to eat, and out in the barn were her friends, the animals, with no special treats.

"Maybe the goats are hungry," said Holly. "I bet Zip and Domingo are, too. May I go out and see how they are?" she asked Mrs. Johnson.

"Yes, of course. Turn on the porch light."

When Holly had put on her blue jacket, the farmer's wife gave her a few doughnuts in a bag and added, "Don't forget to close the barn door when you come out."

Holly hurried outside and into the barn. Zip ran to greet her and the goats had stopped bleating. She gave each of them a piece of doughnut, then fed the rest to Zip and Domingo.

The collie nuzzled against Holly as she stroked Domingo's ears. "Good night, my pets," she said.

Zip trotted at her heels to the door. When Holly opened it, she heard something move in the darkness near the chicken run.

"Come with me, Zip," she whispered. The big

dog bounded at her side as Holly raced across the yard and burst into the house.

"What's the matter?" Pete asked.

"I think there's something hiding out by the barn," said Holly breathlessly.

Ricky snorted. "Scaredy Cat."

"Well, there was," insisted Holly.

"Girls!" said Ricky, looking superior. "Always afraid of the dark."

"Mrs. Johnson," said Holly, "may Zip sleep in our room tonight? I think he's—he's lonesome."

"Of course, dear." Within half an hour Pam and Holly were tucked into bed with Zip on the floor beside them.

In the middle of the night, the collie suddenly began to bark.

"Hush!" ordered Holly. "Lie down before you wake everybody up." Zip whined, but obeyed, and all was quiet until daylight. Next morning when the children went to feed the animals, Pete found the barn door ajar.

"Look!" he exclaimed, hastening toward the stalls. "One of the goats is missing."

CHAPTER 11

THE RIGHT TRAIL

"Holly," said Pete sternly, "you must have left the barn door open last night."

"Honest, I didn't!"

"Then how did the goat get loose?" Ricky asked.

"Instead of arguing," Pam said softly, "I think we should search."

While Holly and Ricky circled the barn, Pete and Pam climbed the frosty slope to the edge of the woods. In the distance below, several white ducks moved slowly over the pond toward the grove of willows at the water's edge. A rooster crowed, and Pete and Pam stopped to listen, their breath coming in white puffs.

Just then, they saw Ricky and Holly come around the barn in their blue and red jackets, and at the same time a faint bleating sound drifted up the slope.

"What was that?" Pete exclaimed.

"The goat."

"Look. Ricky's pointing toward the pond."

"I can't see anything," Pam replied, squinting.

"Maybe the goat's in the willow grove. Come on!"

Pete and Pam raced down the hill, reaching the pond moments behind Ricky and Holly.

"The noise came from around here," said Ricky, scratching his head, "but where's the goat?"

Just then, the bleating sounded directly over their heads! Startled, the children looked up and saw a small goat lashed onto a branch several feet above them.

"Oh!" exclaimed Pam. "You poor thing!"

With Ricky's help, Pete climbed up and untied the animal. Carefully he handed it down to the three pairs of upraised arms.

"There's a note on its collar," said Pam, as they set the goat on his legs again. She opened a piece of paper and read the scrawled message: THIS IS WHAT YOU GET FOR SCARING US!

"Joey and Will!" declared Ricky. "They must have heard us laughing after our trick."

"So that's why the animals were disturbed last night," Pete said. "Joey and Will must have been snooping around the barn, before they took the goat."

"Joey just can't wait for mischief night, I guess," Pam remarked, as she steered the wobbly goat toward the barn door.

"Every night is mischief night for him," Ricky said, "but we'll show him!"

After the animals had been fed, the Hollisters changed clothes and went to church with the

Johnsons. Later, during dinner, Pete sat quietly. Finally, he said, "Mr. Johnson, if Pam and I could go to Clareton today, I think we might learn whether or not it's any use to go on searching for the golden witch."

"How so?"

"If Yagar really did saw off the black-witch weather vane, he probably lost no time in opening it to see if the treasure was inside."

"You mean he cut it apart then and there?" the farmer asked.

"That's a good guess, Pete," Mrs. Johnson put in admiringly. "Will you have some more fudge cake, Ricky?"

The red-haired boy held his plate forward and another wedge was dropped upon it.

Mr. Johnson tapped a spoon against his tea saucer thoughtfully. "You feel that the pieces are still there?"

"Yes. And if we find them, we'll be able to tell whether it was the golden witch painted black. If it is, Yagar has the treasure."

"But if it's just a black-iron witch, we can go on hunting," said Pam.

Holly frowned. "But what about the mysterious package up in the barn? When are we going to get that down?"

"Yikes!" Ricky spluttered. "We forgot about that."

"All but me," replied Holly, thrusting out her lip.

"No problem," said Mrs. Johnson. "I'll drive Pete and Pam to Clareton while the rest of you poke into that mysterious package."

Half an hour later, Mrs. Johnson parked her car in Doyster Street. Pete and Pam hastened to the weed-grown lot of the house on the corner.

Pam eyed a sturdy rose trellis that went nearly to the roof. "That must be how the thief climbed up," she observed.

While Mrs. Johnson looked on, the youngsters pushed into the high grass to a hedge and slipped through it into the yard. It was equally unkempt.

Pete and Pam moved back and forth like hound dogs on the trail of a rabbit. Finally Pam spotted a piece of black iron.

"It's half the witch!" she cried out, holding her find high in the air.

"And here's the other half!" cried Pete. The boy flicked out the blade of his pocketknife and scraped the surface of the weather vane. Although he scratched in several places, no gold appeared beneath the black!

"The hunt's still on!" Pam cried out happily, and the two children danced about like Indians.

After leaving the sawed-apart weather vane at the Clareton police station, the young sleuths drove back to the farm with Mrs. Johnson.

They found Ricky, Holly, Zip, and the farmer sitting on the living-room floor amid a mess of scattered old newspapers. Holly was holding a big scrapbook in her lap.

"*It's half the witch!*"

"All this stuff was in the bundle!" Ricky sang out. He held up a yellowed newspaper with a headline reading: LINDY FLIES OCEAN.

"Adam Cornwall saved newspapers with historical headlines," Mr. Johnson said, rising to his feet.

"And this is his scrapbook," said Holly. "It has a lot of clippings about boats Mr. Cornwall sailed on.

"He used to be a sailor," said the farmer.

"Did you find any clues?" asked Pete, as he and Pam knelt beside their sister.

Holly shook her head. "I guess not. There's nothing about a treasure or a flying compass."

"Listen to this," said Pam, and read a clipping aloud. It told how the seaman had dived into the shark-infested Indian Ocean to rescue a drowning man, who turned out to be a maharajah.

"Yikes! That's like a king, isn't it?" said Ricky, and Pam nodded.

"Adam Cornwall must have been very brave," Pete remarked. "The maharajah was lucky."

"And what luck did you have with the witch?" Mr. Johnson asked.

"Good luck!" Pam told the story while the children tidied the room and made the papers and scrapbook into a neat bundle.

"Maybe we'll find a good clue at Bunny's tonight," said Holly. That reminded Pete to call his father and ask him to pick the children up at the deer farm at nine o'clock instead of at the Johnson farm.

After a delicious supper, Mrs. Johnson helped the children into their jackets and hugged them all.

"Thank you both so much," Pam said. "You're helping us to solve an awful hard mystery."

"We loved having you, and I hope you can untangle the whole riddle," the woman said, as they carried their overnight cases onto the back porch. Zip followed at their heels, his tail waving.

"Mrs. Johnson," said Holly, "is it all right if we take Zip home for a little visit?"

"Certainly. You take him."

"We'll bring him back tomorrow," Holly promised, as she and Zip climbed into the back seat of the farmer's car.

"May we take some apples to the mill then?" Ricky asked, and was assured that he could.

At Bunny's house, the porch light was on, and she ushered her callers into her cozy home.

"Now take your jackets off," Bunny said, "and we'll get right to work on your mystery." She pointed to a row of old ledgers standing on the desk in the corner. "I dug them out of the attic this morning."

Each of the Hollisters took a thick book and began looking for an entry that might show who had paid for the golden witch.

"I wish I knew when it was made," Bunny said with a sigh, "but I don't, so we'll have to go through the books until we find the right place."

"Crickets," said Pete, "this old-fashioned handwriting is hard to read."

They found a number of sales of black-iron witches, but none of a vane covered with gold leaf. For a long time they paged through the books until they became weary.

Suddenly the silence was broken as Zip jumped up and ran to the door, barking.

"What's the matter with him?" asked Pete.

"Maybe there's somebody out there," said Bunny.

Pam looked up, frowning, then back at her ledger.

The other children and Bunny went to the barking dog, but Pam continued to puzzle over the cramped handwriting.

Pete held Zip by the collar as Bunny opened the door. The light from the living room streamed out, but beyond it lay darkness. Zip strained forward and growled.

"Let him go," said Ricky. "If there's a prowler out there, Zip'll catch him."

"No!" exclaimed Holly. "Zip might get hurt!"

Before Ricky could answer, Pam cried out excitedly. "The witch! Here it is! I've found it!"

CHAPTER 12

NOBODY HOME!

AT PAM's exclamation, Bunny and the others spun around, dumfounded.

"It's in here!" Pam cried. "The record of the sale! The golden witch was bought by Phineas Cobb of Shoreham."

"You're fooling!" said Ricky as he closed the door.

"Phinny who?" asked Holly as they crouched around Pam.

"Phineas Cobb," Pam repeated. "Look here."

Thin, scrawly handwriting recorded that the witch was covered with gold leaf and that there was an extra charge for enclosing an object in the weather vane.

"That's the right one," declared Pete. "Crickets! Our best clue yet."

"Phineas Cobb might not be living now," Pam went on, "but maybe we can find his family. Do you know any Cobbs, Bunny?"

"No, but Grandfather may. I'll inquire when I see him on Tuesday."

"Isn't he home yet?" Holly spoke up impa-

112

tiently, and glanced at Bunny's telephone on a nearby desk.

The deer lady explained that her grandfather would not be back until Monday night. "Tuesday morning is the first time I'll be able to reach him."

"That's okay," said Pete. "We can start working on the clue right now if you'll let us use your telephone."

"Help yourself," said Bunny. "I'll get refreshments." She vanished into the kitchen. When she returned with cookies and milk, Pete was at the desk with the others crowded around him.

"We found four Cobbs in the telephone book," Pam announced.

"Pete called two of 'em," said Ricky, "but they were the wrong ones."

"Shh!" said Holly as Pete signaled for silence. "He's got another one."

Breathlessly the children listened as their brother asked if this was the family of Phineas Cobb. They heard a laugh at the other end of the line, a raspy reply and the receiver click.

"What did he say?" asked Holly.

Pete made a face. "He said, 'No Phineas Cobb lives here, but we've got his brother Corn Cobb.'"

Everybody groaned.

"Some corny joker," said Ricky.

"Oh *no!*" exclaimed Holly and tried to tickle Ricky. Giggling, the two scuffled around a chair.

"Cut it out," said Pete. "We're not through yet."

"There's one more number," Pam reminded them. "It might be the right one."

Once again Pete called, but this time there was no answer.

"We'll have to try again tomorrow," he said as he hung up.

"We're so near and yet so far," said Pam with a sigh. "I can hardly wait."

While the youngsters pondered over the treasure in the weather vane, Bunny fed them oatmeal cookies and milk. Ricky had finished his last "extra" cookie by the time Mr. Hollister drove up.

Next morning Sue was first down for breakfast. Holly skipped to the table and hugged her little sister. "Did you and Mother make a costume for the Halloween party?"

"Oh, yes!"

"Let's see it."

"We burned it up."

"Oh, Sue," said Pam, pulling up her chair. "You know that isn't so."

"Yes, it is," insisted the little girl. "We burned it. Didn't we, Mommy?"

"That's right. Every scrap."

"Didn't you like it?" asked Ricky, wrinkling his freckled nose.

"We liked it very much," said Mrs. Hollister as she put hot buttered toast on the table. "And you might as well not ask any more questions because that's all we're going to tell you."

"This is some kind of a joke," Ricky declared, but Sue only smiled sweetly.

The children were puzzled all the way to school, but could not figure out the strange double-talk at the breakfast table.

When they reached the play yard, Joey Brill and Will Wilson were standing at the corner of the building, waiting for them.

"Hi," said Joey. "We want to tell you something."

"Maybe we don't want to hear it," said Pete coolly.

"You ought to be ashamed," Pam declared, "putting that poor goat up in the tree."

Will grinned. "Can't you take a joke?"

"It's not funny to hurt an animal," Holly said hotly.

"Well, we're sorry," said Joey. "What we wanted to tell you is that we've decided to come to your party."

"Yes," Will chimed in. "We figured we ought to be more friendly."

The Hollisters were taken aback and looked at the bullies in amazement.

"Very well," Pam said finally. "We invited you and won't go back on our invitation."

"But we're warning you," Pete said. "No more mean tricks."

Later at recess Pam and Holly told Ann Hunter what had happened at the farm and about Joey's surprise acceptance.

"Ann, what do you suppose is the real reason they changed their minds?" Pam asked.

"I don't know. Maybe Jeff can tell us. There he is now. Oh, Jeff!"

The lad came running. He had a ready answer to his sister's question. "Sure, I know. Joey and Will want to come to the party because Jimmy Cox told everybody there were going to be big prizes."

"Why did Jimmy do that?" Pam asked, showing some annoyance.

"I don't know. All I told him was that Holly said your father was going to give Scout knives to the boys."

"Scout knives!" Holly's face flushed with indignation. "I never told you that, Jeff! I said 'Wait and see.'"

"How stories do grow," Pam said breezily.

At noon the Hollisters hurried home, impatient to call the number that had not answered the night before. This time a woman was at home. She told Pam that there had been no one by that name in her family.

"We have a Philip and a Francis," she said with amusement in her voice, "but no Phineas, I'm sorry to say."

"Thank you," Pam said. The girl hung up and frowned. "There must be some other Cobbs around. We can ask Aunt Nettie and the Johnsons if they know any."

After school Holly and Ricky raced home first, eager to start for the farm. Pete and Pam followed to find a police car parked in front of the Hollister property. Ricky and Holly were standing next to it, leaning in the window on the driver's side.

"Crickets," said Pete, "I wonder what's up!" He and Pam ran to the car and saw that the big attraction was their friend, Officer Cal.

"Pete, I hear you almost got arrested in Clareton," the young policeman said with a grin.

"It was close! Thanks for identifying me."

"We told him all about the ledger already," put in Holly.

"Do you know some Cobbs?" Pete asked the policeman.

"I know two maiden ladies named Cobb who live about a mile up the road from Aunt Nettie's Cider Mill."

"That's wonderful!" exclaimed Pam. "I guess they don't have a phone, do they?"

Officer Cal shook his head. "No." Then he offered to drive the children to the farm, since he had to make a trip that way. Pete and Pam hurried into the house to leave their books.

When Mrs. Hollister heard where they were going, she said, "There's an empty cider jug in the back vestibule. Please return it to Mr. Johnson."

Pam called Zip and they ran back to the car. As four children and the dog piled in, Officer Cal grinned. "Good thing I'm not driving a motorcycle today."

On the way, the policeman was brought up to

date on all the latest clues. He listened carefully, then said, "We'll try to track down Yagar."

"I wonder if he'll get in touch with us again," said Pete.

"I hope not," replied the officer. "He may be dangerous. Well, here's the farm."

The children found Mr. Johnson outside the barn putting a carton of empty cider jugs into Domingo's cart. Zip barked joyfully at the burro, then ran off to play with the goats in the pasture.

While Pete helped the farmer load baskets of apples, he told him that they wanted to visit the Cobbs and explained why.

"All right," Mr. Johnson said as Pam put her cider jug in the carton. "But don't stay too long." The children climbed aboard, Mr. Johnson slapped Domingo's rump, and they were off.

As the cart bumped over the road through the woods, Holly said happily, "Soon we'll know where the golden witch is!"

"Don't be too sure," cautioned Pete. "This might not be the right Cobb family." But he had to admit that he was excited over the new lead.

When they reached the mill, Pete and Ricky carried the apple baskets to the shed, while Pam and Holly toted the jugs inside. There stood Aunt Nettie, sleeves rolled up, in front of a big barrel, filling cider jugs.

"Can't stop!" she called to them. "I have two dozen more to fill." She held a jug under a faucet on the barrel, turned the handle, and out came a stream of amber cider. "Glad to see you brought empties," she added.

"Apples, too," said Ricky.

"Good," boomed the woman. "How would you like some cider? Get those big mugs from the shelf by the door."

"Thank you, but we can't stay," said Pam.

"I'll stay," offered Ricky, going for a mug.

"So will I," said Holly, following him. "May we help you fill bottles? I'd love to turn that little faucet off and on."

It was agreed that the younger children would work with Aunt Nettie, while Pete and Pam drove to the Cobbs'.

"The place is easy to find," Aunt Nettie told them, filling Holly's mug. "It's a dark-green house with white shutters, on the left side of the road. There's a little farm attached to it."

"I wonder why Bunny didn't know about the Cobbs," said Ricky, watching his mug fill up.

"He means Miss Bunting," Pam said to Aunt Nettie.

"Little Bunting grew up on the other side of Shoreham," said the big woman. "She's only lived out this way for six months. Besides," she added with a smile, "the Cobb sisters keep pretty much to themselves."

Pete and Pam hurried off, wondering what the Cobbs would be like. Pete took the reins and, after riding about a mile, the children saw the green

"May we help you?" Holly asked.

house. Pete halted Domingo in front of the porch and they went to the door.

As Pete raised his hand to ring the bell, a voice shouted, "Go away!" Pete and Pam exchanged startled looks. The voice seemed to have come from behind the curtained window beside the door.

Pam went close to it and called, "We're not selling anything. We just want to talk!"

"Nobody home!" came the raucous voice.

"Wait a minute," Pete whispered. He put his eye to the window and peered between the curtains. "It's a parrot!"

Pam peeked in, too, and saw a big red and green bird in a cage.

Pete rang the doorbell several times, then decided that the parrot was right. Nobody was at home.

Disappointed, they climbed back into the cart and headed for the mill, where they found Ricky and Holly waiting at the door with Aunt Nettie.

She shooed the younger children toward the cart. "Go straight home," she called to Pete. "It's getting late. You shouldn't be going through the woods after dark."

Pete promised to make haste and they drove off. By the time they reached the top of the rise, daylight was nearly gone. A few birds still twittered overhead, but as they went downhill on the other side, the woods grew silent. The trees loomed up like dark giants on either side of the narrow road. Gradually, the children talked less, and secretly hated to think of passing Farmer Johnson's old barn.

As they drew near it, a figure suddenly stepped into their path.

"Halt!" said a harsh voice.

CHAPTER 13

TRADING SECRETS

"Mr. Curie-Us!" Pete exclaimed as the man jumped in front of the cart. "You scared us!"

"Good," Yagar replied unpleasantly. "I want you to know I mean business about that witch. Have you found it yet?"

"No, sir."

"We thought perhaps *you* had," Pam spoke up.

"What do you mean?"

The Hollisters told him about the weather vane that had been taken from the house in Clareton.

"I don't know anything about that," Yagar replied. Then, in a confidential voice, he went on:

"Look, for certain reasons, I can't do a lot of snooping about the vane myself, but you kids can and nobody'll think anything of it. Now why don't you get busy and earn your money?"

"All right," said Pete, playing his part well. "But suppose we do locate the witch. Where can we find you?"

"You can't. But I can reach you whenever I want. You'll hear from me in a couple of days."

Abruptly he stepped back and hurried off into the dark woods.

For a moment the children sat quietly, still shaken by their fright.

"Yikes," said Ricky, "he's really spying on us!"

"Giddap, Domingo," cried Pete, and on they went.

When the children reached the barn, they related their adventure to Mr. Johnson. "That does it!" the farmer said emphatically. "No more cart trips!"

"But we have to go at least once more," Pete begged, "because the Cobbs weren't home today."

"We'll see what your parents say," the farmer replied. He drove his helpers to their home, stepped inside, and talked with Mr. and Mrs. Hollister. The children listened eagerly.

Then Pete said, "I don't think Yagar will bother us again for a while. He has to give us time to look for the witch."

"All right," Mr. Hollister said finally, "only one more trip to the other side of the hill."

"But see that you are back before dark," their mother cautioned. "And thank you, Mr. Johnson, for being so concerned about my angels."

"Angels, ugh!" Ricky said, and Mr. Johnson laughed.

"Then we'll see your detectives tomorrow." He shook hands with Mr. Hollister and drove away.

Next morning the youngsters started off for school, anticipating the afternoon visit to the Cobb sisters. Besides, Ricky was cooking up a plan of his own. At noon he hurried home for lunch, and when it was over he took two apples and raced outside to the garage. There he dragged a metal tub onto the grass, hosed it full of water, and dropped the apples in. After that, Ricky sat on the front steps, waiting for Jeff Hunter to pass by.

As soon as the Hunter boy appeared, Ricky called to him, "How'd you like to duck for apples?"

"Swell."

Ricky led him to the tub. "Go ahead. Company first."

As Jeff was about to kneel, he glanced up and saw Holly watching from the porch. She shook her head and Jeff hesitated. "You go on, Ricky," he said. "Show me."

"Oh, it's easy," declared Ricky. He dropped to his knees and lowered his face to the water. Holly raced across the yard like lightning, and before Ricky knew what was going on, she pushed his head into the water.

As the redhead came up sputtering, Jeff laughed and Holly burst into giggles. "Ha-ha-ha! You got fooled," she said.

"Who did it?" Ricky stormed.

Jeff and Holly looked at each other innocently.

"A Halloween spook, I guess," said Holly.

Ricky pursed his lips and ran off into the house to get dried. As he toweled his head, he vowed to work the trick on somebody *sometime!*

That afternoon the Hollisters rode their bicycles to school and pedaled straight to the farm afterward.

Holly pushed Ricky's head into the water.

Mr. Johnson had Domingo and the cart waiting for them outside the barn and they started off at once for the Cobbs'.

"Don't forget," the farmer called. "Be back before dark."

As Domingo plodded along the woodland road, Holly bounced on the seat.

"Oh," she said, "I wish we could go faster!"

"So do I," said Pam. Her eyes were bright with excitement.

"Wait till we hit the road," Pete promised.

As they passed the cider mill, he shook the reins and the burro broke into a brisk trot.

"Forward, men," shouted Ricky, "we're on our way to break this case!"

"*We hope*," Pete cautioned with a grin. "Don't pop your top yet."

When they reached the small green and white house, Pete stopped the cart in the side yard. Ricky was last as they hurried around to the front porch. Passing under a maple tree, he heard a hissing sound and glanced up. On a high branch was a large gray cat, glaring down at him.

The other children paid no attention, for they had seen the curtain on the front window suddenly drop into place.

"Someone was peeking out," Holly whispered at the foot of the porch steps.

Pete led the way up the stairs and rang the bell. The curtain stirred. No one came to the door. He rang again. Finally the handle rattled and the door opened cautiously.

A slender woman in a pink cotton dress looked out. Her white hair was piled high on her head in soft curls. Bright brown eyes looked shyly at them.

"Miss Cobb?" said Pete.

"Ye-es?" she asked. "What is it?" She spoke very softly and slowly.

"We'd like to talk to you, please," said Pete. He introduced himself and the others.

"Who is it?" came a high piping voice from inside.

The woman at the door turned her head. "Some children. They want to talk to us."

"Please," put in Pam. "It's very urgent."

"Well—all right," said the woman in pink. "Come in." She opened the door wider and when the Hollisters were inside, she closed it carefully. Then she led them through an archway into the living room.

It was crowded with old-fashioned furniture, and the lamp shades were covered with fringed shawls. In front of the window was a big brass cage containing the red and green parrot. Next to it stood a small woman with short, straight gray hair and silver-rimmed spectacles.

"Are they the ones who did the trick?" she piped.

The woman in pink frowned at them. "Did you come here last night and prop our ladder up to the barn roof?"

"Halloween jokes are all right," put in the gray-haired woman, "but it won't be so funny for us, getting that big ladder down again."

The Hollisters' mouths were agape at the accusation.

"Oh, no, we didn't play any trick on you," Pam said.

An idea crossed Pete's mind, but he kept it to himself. Instead, he said, "We'll take the ladder down for you."

The two ladies looked at each other. "I don't believe they did the trick," said the one in pink.

"No, you look like nice children," remarked the other. "What are your names?"

Pete told her.

"I'm Miss Delora Cobb," said the woman in pink, "and this is my sister, Miss Sylvia."

"Nobody home," announced the parrot, and the youngsters chuckled.

The ladies invited their callers to take off their jackets and sit down. Then Miss Delora went to the window and opened the curtains. After a quick look out, she seated herself on the sofa beside her sister.

"Any sign?" Miss Sylvia asked her softly.

The other shook her head slightly. "No."

Holly and Ricky could not help looking puzzled, but Pete and Pam politely pretended not to have heard.

Pete cleared his throat and launched into the story of the golden witch. Then he said, "We would like to know if you are any relation to Phineas Cobb."

The two women exchanged cautious glances, and Miss Delora said slowly, "He was our uncle."

"Oh, how lucky!" exclaimed Pam. "You are the right Cobbs!"

"Do you know where the golden witch is?" Pete asked eagerly.

"No-oo," replied Miss Delora in her slow soft way.

"Oh," said Pam in disappointment. "But maybe you could give us a clue, anyhow. Did your uncle ever mention anything about the golden witch?"

"Oh, yes, of course," said the woman in pink. "We know the secret of the witch, don't we, Sylvia?"

Her sister had turned around to gaze anxiously toward the window. "Yes, indeed," she replied. "We overheard it as children."

"It will do no harm to tell you about that," Miss Delora went on. "Sylvia and I were playing house behind the draperies in the parlor when Uncle Phineas came and told our father all about it. We couldn't help hearing."

"You see," said Miss Sylvia, "Uncle Phineas was only the middle man. He bought the witch for a man who didn't want anyone to know who had it."

"It was no one in our family," added Miss Delora.

"Did your uncle say who the man was?" Pete asked.

"Oh, yes," chorused the Cobbs.

"Who?" Ricky burst out.

The two ladies looked surprised. "Goodness," said Miss Delora gently, "we can't tell you that."

"No," said her sister, "*that* part is the secret."

The sisters explained that their father had found them behind the draperies and made them promise never to tell the name of the man who had ordered the witch.

"We never have," said Miss Delora.

"And we never will," her sister added firmly.

The Hollisters were speechless with disappointment, and Pam's eyes filled with tears. "Oh dear," she thought, "just when we were so close!"

Miss Delora stood up. "Now you'll have to run along, children, because we must look for our cat. He's been missing several hours. You've probably noticed that my sister and I are very worried. We must find him."

"If we only knew *where* to look," said Miss Sylvia unhappily.

Ricky spoke up. "I know where he is."

"Oh," cried Miss Delora, "where?"

The boy took a deep breath. "It's a secret. I'll trade it for your secret."

"Ricky!" Pam said in a scolding voice.

Even Pete eyed his brother sternly. "You'd better tell," he advised.

"I'll tell if they'll tell," Ricky replied stubbornly.

"You can't do that, Ricky," Pam said. "It's not nice."

131

Ricky's face grew as red as his hair. "Well, whoever bought the witch must have died long ago. It doesn't matter to him any more, but it does matter to us."

His words poured out as he looked at Pam. "You and Pete have worked hard to find the witch and keep that mean man from getting it!"

He turned to the Cobb sisters. "Pam was even crying she felt so bad!" Ricky stopped talking and bit his lip. His eyes filled with hot tears.

As the Cobbs looked at him in gentle amazement, Ricky hung his head. "Never mind," he blurted out. "I'm sorry." He turned toward the door. "I'll get your cat for you."

"Wait!" Miss Sylvia said.

"The boy is right!" added Miss Delora. "We'll tell you."

Ricky whirled. "Yikes!" he exploded happily.

Amid the Hollisters' delighted thanks, Ricky dashed outside. From the window, the others saw him scramble up the tree trunk until he grasped the lower branch. He disappeared upward, but tumbling red and yellow leaves showed his progress.

Fifteen minutes later he reappeared and hung from the bottom branch, grasping a large struggling cat. Then he dropped about six feet to the ground as the Cobb sisters gasped.

"What a brave boy!" exclaimed Miss Sylvia.

"You were just splendid, young man," cried Miss Delora as Ricky came in, scratched and stuck with bits of bark and leaves.

"Now we'll tell you our secret," said Miss Sylvia.

"Henry Cobb!" exclaimed Miss Delora happily as she took the cat from Ricky.

The Hollisters looked puzzled. "Is that the man's name?" Pam asked.

"Dear me, no!" exclaimed Miss Sylvia. "Henry Cobb is our cat. The man who bought the witch was Adam Cornwall."

CHAPTER 14

A RECKLESS RIDER

As ONE voice, the children shouted, "Adam Cornwall?"

The sisters looked surprised. "You know about him?" Miss Sylvia asked.

After another chorus of excited answers, Pete poured out the entire story of the mysterious tombstone with the winged compass, and their search for the golden witch.

The spinsters beamed with pleasure at their part in untangling the mystery.

"Was the golden witch on the old barn?" Pam asked.

"Yes, indeed," replied Miss Delora, "but it vanished during a big storm." Many years before, she explained, lightning had struck the barn and caused part of the roof to collapse.

"Oh, the thunder!" said Miss Sylvia. "It was frightening."

"I always said the storm was too much for Adam Cornwall," Miss Delora continued. "The poor old man died that very night."

"What happened to the weather vane?" asked Holly.

The sisters said they did not know.

"Maybe Mr. Cornwall's heirs found it," said Pete.

"Dear me, no," replied Miss Sylvia. "He had no family left." She explained that the next owner of the farm had been Mr. Johnson.

"But he hasn't found the witch!" exclaimed Pete. "It must still be there!"

"And what do you think the treasure is?" Miss Sylvia asked.

"Maybe the compass," Pam guessed.

"Crickets! How could that be a treasure?" Pete said.

"Oh dear, dear," Miss Delora said, stroking Henry Cobb in her lap. "All your hard detective work for an old compass."

Suddenly the parrot began squawking and flapping around the cage in fright. All eyes went to the window, where a young deer gazed in at them.

The cat shot off Miss Delora's lap and landed on the bird cage, hissing at the deer. The sisters screamed.

"Go away!" cried Miss Sylvia fluttering her arms toward the window. The deer bounded off.

"That's Ambrose!" Holly cried.

"Sure. He's loose again," exclaimed Ricky. "Come on! We'll get him."

The younger children grabbed their jackets and

The cat shot off her lap.

ran for the door. "We'll meet you at the cider mill!" cried Holly.

"Okay!" said Pete, who by this time was helping Pam to lift the cat off the bird cage. But Henry Cobb streaked from their grasp, leaped to the floor, and slunk under the sofa.

"Now he'll never come out!" Miss Delora said with a big sigh.

"I'll get him," Pete volunteered. He wriggled under the sofa, coaxed the cat quietly, and presently emerged with Henry Cobb, purring contentedly.

"Thank you," Miss Sylvia said. "You're kind children to help us."

"We're not used to much excitement," Miss Delora confessed, as Pete and Pam donned their jackets.

"Be sure to let us know if you find the golden witch," said Miss Delora.

Her sister plucked Pam's sleeve. "The ladder, dear," she whispered. "Put it in the barn."

The youngsters promised to do both, thanked the Cobbs, and left.

They walked into the backyard past a hencoop to a small barn. Against one wall leaned a wooden ladder. Close to it was a long-handled water pump.

"Watch out," Pam said. "It's muddy here."

As Pete placed his hands on the ladder, he glanced down.

"Pam—look!"

In the mud were several perfect footprints—

made by a small flat-heeled shoe with a pointed toe.

"They look like a man's," Pam said, studying the prints.

"Yes," Pete replied, "and guess who wears pointed shoes—Yagar!"

Pam's face clouded. "Oh, how awful! He found out about the Cobbs, and it's all my fault. He must have been the prowler outside Bunny's house and heard me say the name."

Pete glanced up at the barn. "I guess Yagar figured there was a weather vane here, and it broke off and might be lying on the roof."

Together the children lifted the ladder and carried it into the barn. The Cobb sisters smilingly waved their thanks from a window.

"Do you think we ought to tell them about the footprints?" Pam asked.

"No. They'd only get frightened. Besides, I doubt if Yagar will come back here again."

In the waning daylight Pete and Pam drove down the deserted road toward the mill. As Domingo plodded along, Pete and Pam kept their eyes peeled for Ricky, Holly, and the deer, but did not see them.

Suddenly a roaring noise came toward the children. Startled, they stared ahead. Coming directly at them out of the dusk was a motorcycle without lights!

"It's going to hit us!" Pam shrieked.

Pete tried to pull Domingo off the road, but the frightened burro broke into a trot.

All at once the motorcyclist put on an extra burst of speed that made a deafening racket as the vehicle swerved past the donkey cart. In panic, Domingo leaped into the field by the side of the road and raced through a patch of corn stubble.

"Wait! Stop!" cried Pete, clinging tightly to the reins. The cart swayed and pitched, nearly throwing Pam out, before it came to a halt in the middle of the field.

Pam jumped out and stroked the shaking burro. "There, there," Pam said kindly. "Everything's all right now."

"Lucky we didn't break a wheel," Pete remarked. With Pam holding the bridle and Pete the reins, the children guided their pet back to the road.

The reckless driver was not in sight, nor could they hear the sound of his motor.

"Signal green," Pete said with a grin. "Away to the cider mill."

"What a wild driver that was," Pam said as Domingo clip-clopped along. "Did you see what he looked like, Pete?"

"No. He came too fast."

When they arrived at the deer farm, Bunny was busy feeding her animals.

"Did Ricky and Holly bring Ambrose back?" Pete called out.

"No. I haven't seen them."

The words brought a sinking feeling to Pam. "I

hope they're not still chasing him," she thought.

"We have some good news which we'll tell you later," Pete said loudly to Bunny, and waved good-by.

The cart stopped next before the cider mill. Ricky and Holly were not there.

"I haven't seen 'em," Aunt Nettie said. "But I heard their voices in the woods. It sounded as if they were heading up the slope."

Pete felt relieved to hear this. "They must have gone back to the farm," he remarked.

As the cart creaked up the hill, Pam said, "I think it would be nice to invite Aunt Nettie and Bunny to our party."

"Yes, and Bunny's grandfather, too," Pete agreed. "But we'll just ask them," he added, "'cause it's too late to make any more invitations. Halloween's day after tomorrow."

Pam gave a happy sigh. "I can hardly wait."

"And I can hardly wait to find that witch," Pete declared.

Pam smiled. "It's certainly been a good-news day!"

"Everything will be cleared up by spook night," Pete said gaily, but nevertheless kept his eyes peeled for any movement in the dark woods surrounding the lonely lane. If Curie-Us should spring out at them now, what would they say in answer to his questions? They would have to tell the truth about the golden witch.

Pete's nerves finally relaxed after Domingo passed the old barn.

When Pete and Pam reached the Johnsons', they were bubbling with happy thoughts. Quickly they unhitched Domingo and put the cart away. Then they raced eagerly toward the farmhouse.

As they burst into the kitchen, pink-faced and beaming, Mr. and Mrs. Johnson looked relieved.

"There you are at last!" the woman said.

"Mr. Johnson," Pete said breathlessly, "how does it feel to have a treasure on your farm?"

But the farm couple's faces clouded. They seemed not to have heard the question.

Mr. Johnson spoke sternly. "Where are Ricky and Holly?"

CHAPTER 15

LITTLE BOBBILY THINGS

AT THAT very moment, high on the wooded slope, Ricky and Holly paused to look down into a small hollow. Dimly they could see the shape of a little deer.

"There he is," Holly said, panting. "There's Ambrose."

Quietly the brother and sister made their way down the slope. The deer turned his head to watch them approach, but did not move.

A few feet away from the animal, Ricky thrust his hand forward and grasped the deer's chain.

"I've got him."

"Nice Ambrose," said Holly. The deer licked her hand.

"He's tired," she said.

"So am I," said Ricky. "Yikes, did we run!"

Half-stumbling, the children led the fawn up out of the hollow. They decided to go straight to the Johnsons' farm and return the deer to Bunny the next day.

"It's dark," said Ricky guiltily. "Everybody'll be wondering where we are."

"Yes," said Holly. "We're going to be in trouble and it's your fault, Ambrose."

The deer walked docilely beside the children and stopped when Holly did. "Which way is the farm, Ricky?" she asked.

Her brother scratched his head. "Is it that way?" He pointed left.

"I'm asking you," Holly replied. "I don't know."

"I don't either," Ricky admitted. "We crisscrossed so much." The children stood silent, looking for a familiar sign. Somewhere they could hear water gurgling, but there was no break in the trees. A sudden sharp wind blew a swirl of leaves around them, and the pines moaned and sighed. Holly held the ends of her sleeves closed, and shivered.

Ricky tried to stick his hands in his jacket pockets, but they were stuffed with corks.

"What are we going to do?" Holly asked.

"Let me think a minute," her brother said, trying to keep his voice from trembling.

"We're lost," Holly whispered, and began to cry. "They'll never find us!"

Suddenly Ricky had an idea. "Don't cry. I know what we can do!"

"What?" Holly tried to stifle her sobs.

Ricky took his sister's hand. "Bring Ambrose, and come on," he said. "I've got a plan."

Meanwhile, at the farm, Pete had telephoned his home and the houses of the Hollisters' friends to see if the younger children were there. When they could not be found, a search party was organized

143

by telephone. Within fifteen minutes headlights began to sweep up the Johnsons' drive and the searchers parked their cars in the farmyard.

Officer Cal arrived with two other policemen, whom he introduced as Roberts and Mullaney. They took Pete and Pam to one side and asked rapid-fire questions.

Where were Ricky and Holly seen last? In what direction were they going? Were they familiar with the woods? Did they carry flashlights?

When all the questions had been answered, Pete left the officers to join his parents who were talking with the Hunters and the Meads. Sue was clinging to her mother's hand.

"How do you think we should search?" Mr. Mead asked.

Officer Cal supplied the answer. "We'll climb the hill in teams." He looked about the assembled faces and added, "Roberts and Mullaney; Pam and Dave Mead; Pete and Ann Hunter; Jeff goes with his father; Meads and Johnsons together."

The policeman took a breath and scanned the crowd again. "Who's left? Oh, yes." He assigned Mrs. Hunter and the Martins as a team, including Donna, whose red eyes showed she had been crying.

"All right, Mr. and Mrs. Hollister," he added, "you and Sue come with me."

The teams lined up fifty feet apart. Zip had been brought from the barn and stayed close to Pete.

"Now stick to your partners," Cal instructed loudly. "We don't want anybody else wandering off and getting lost."

While he was speaking, there came the roar of a motor up on the slope. Two headlight beams shot out of the old wagon road and barreled down across the pasture into the yard. With a screech of brakes, a Jeep came to halt among the cars. Aunt Nettie and Bunny climbed out and hurried over to the search party.

"We're going with you," Aunt Nettie boomed. "I can't see worth a hoot, but I can holler loud."

"Okay. You two are a team," said Officer Cal, "but there's one thing I want to warn all of you about. Sometimes people who are lost in the woods get panicky and are unable to think straight. They have been known to run away from their rescuers. We must be careful not to frighten the children away from us."

At his command, the party set out for the woods, each team carrying a flashlight.

While they walked up to the wagon road, Mr. Mead turned his light from side to side, sweeping the slope above and below. When the beam passed over the pond, Sue cried, "Look! There's a lot of little things!"

Mrs. Hollister was too worried to pay much attention. "Ducks, maybe," she said as Sue tugged her hand.

"No, Mommy, lots of little bobbily things."

Mr. Mead heard Sue and flashed the light on the pond again.

"It's nothing, dear," said Mrs. Hollister. "Just a bunch of corks."

But Pete and Pam had seen them, too, and ran up with their partners.

"Those are Ricky's corks!" Pete cried.

"He got them from Aunt Nettie," said Pam excitedly.

"That's right, he did," said the big woman. "Hold up, everybody," she shouted, and the searchers closed in around the pond.

"Those corks weren't in the pond at sundown," Mr. Johnson declared.

Pete pointed to several corks bobbing down the stream that emptied into the pond.

"They're coming from above," he said. "Ricky must have dropped them in the brook to give us a clue. He and Holly are probably somewhere on the edge of that stream!"

"That makes sense," said Officer Cal. "We'll follow the water."

The search party began to climb the slope on each side of the brook. Soon they entered the woods and the going became rougher. Gradually the distance between the teams widened as they detoured around boulders and ravines.

Pam and Dave were in the rear when Dave stopped and beamed his light on a narrow side stream.

"Those are Ricky's corks!" Pete cried.

"Maybe they're up this branch somewhere," he suggested.

"Let's follow it and see," said Pam.

For a while they stumbled along the rocky bank, then the tiny stream disappeared into the ground.

"Well, that's that," said Dave, disappointed.

"Shh," said Pam, "I think I heard something."

They stood listening, but the only sound was the sighing of the wind and the far-off shouts of the other searchers.

Dave started to turn, but Pam caught his sleeve. "Listen! There it is again."

This time Dave heard it, too. There was a crackling of twigs ahead of them.

"Ricky! Holly!" Pam called. But the wind rose, and the children listened in vain for an answering shout.

"Come on," said Dave. "Let's get closer." He set off as fast as he could.

Pam half-ran and stumbled behind him. "Oh," she said shakily, "I hope it's Ricky and Holly."

"Don't get your hopes too high," the boy replied. "It might only be an animal."

Soon they stopped again and listened. Once more they heard the crackling twigs ahead of them. Together, Pam and Dave shouted, "Ricky! Holly!"

The crackling stopped. The children called again. Then the noise started moving away from the searchers.

Pam and Dave exchanged looks. "If it's Ricky

and Holly," Pam said, "they're frightened and running away like Officer Cal was telling us."

Dave agreed that it was possible. "We'll follow as quietly as we can."

For a quarter of an hour the children trailed the sound, trying to be noiseless. Dave kept the flashlight trained on the ground and shaded it with his hand.

Then they found themselves on the old cart road. All was silent.

"Now which way?" whispered Pam.

The answer came from the woods across the road. Leaves and twigs crackled loudly as something moved away fast.

Once more the children took up the chase, slipping amongst the trees. Then Pam caught Dave's arm and pointed ahead. Through the thinning woods could be seen the black hulk of the old barn.

Dave put out his light and the children hastened to the edge of the moonlit clearing.

As they stood listening, there came the clank of metal from inside the barn.

Pam felt a surge of relief. "It must be Ricky and Holly," she declared softly. "No animal could get that door open. It's heavy."

The two hurried across the clearing to the old sagging door. Dave seized the rusty handle with both hands, which made his flashlight clink against it loudly. He pulled the door open.

Pam was about to dart past him when she

stopped short and gasped. Speechless, Dave stood rooted. Moonlight came through the broken roof and fell on the old car. In the driver's seat sat a stiff figure. Without a sound it slowly rose.

CHAPTER 16

LIZZIE'S TRIP

PAM screamed and ran, with Dave close behind
her. They did not stop until they reached the
cart road, where Pam leaned against a tree and
panted.

"I'm sorry, Dave. I shouldn't be such a coward,
but that thing was awful!"

"What about me?" was Dave's reply. "I ran as
fast as you did!"

"It looked like a ghost, but I know it couldn't
have been," Pam said, finally catching her breath.

"It's a real live person," Dave agreed. "We
ought to go back and see who it is."

"I know we should. But my knees are still shaking."

"So're mine. Anyway," Dave added, "the fellow's probably gone by now. You yelled pretty
loud."

Using Dave's flashlight, the boy and girl started
along the cart road to look for the search party.
After a while they heard voices in the woods to
their left, and hastened toward them. Ahead they
could see a cluster of lights beside the stream.

"What is it?" Pam called as she and Dave ran up.

"Shhh!" came several voices.

"Look!" said Pete as the circle of people opened to let them in.

Under a big tree lay Ricky and Holly, fast asleep. The warm, cuddly deer was their pillow.

Mrs. Hollister shook the exhausted children and Zip barked several times before they awoke.

"Mommy!" Holly cried, and flung her arms around her mother.

"Are we glad to see you!" exclaimed Ricky as he got sleepily to his feet and looked around. "Yikes! The whole town's here."

After Mr. and Mrs. Hollister had made sure they were not hurt, Officer Cal said, "Ricky, that was a clever trick, dropping the corks into the stream."

"I'm glad it worked. Holly and I were afraid you wouldn't find 'em."

"Why didn't you just follow the stream down to the pond?" asked Mr. Johnson.

"We thought of it," said Holly, petting Ambrose, "but everything was dark and scary and we kept hearing noises."

"So we thought we'd just crawl up close to this big tree and wait till you found us," Ricky added.

Bunny took hold of Ambrose's collar. "Come along," she said with a sigh. "You've caused enough trouble for one night."

"We had a scare, too," Pam said. As the search

party headed for the cart road, she and Dave told what they had seen in the barn.

When they reached the clearing, everyone waited while Officer Cal and the other policemen searched the ruined building and the woods around it. There was no sign of the intruder.

"I have a hunch it was Yagar," Pete spoke up. "Somehow he must have found out that the golden witch used to be on Cornwall's barn."

"But how?" Pam asked.

"The Cobb sisters would never tell him," Ricky put in. "Yikes, they almost didn't tell us."

"That's right," Pete agreed. Then, seeing the questioning look on the Johnsons' faces, Pete told the farmer and his wife about the treasure.

"Right on our farm!" Mrs. Johnson exclaimed. "How exciting! We'd better start searching tomorrow, because if Yagar knows it's here, he might beat us to it."

"We can't start tomorrow," Pam said, looking worried, "because we have to decorate the barn for the party. And the next day is Halloween, so we won't have time to search then."

Officer Cal chuckled. "I don't think your prowler will look for the witch with all you youngsters running around here."

Pete suggested that they tie Zip outside the old barn until the treasure was found. "He'll bark a warning if Yagar or anybody else comes around," Pete guaranteed.

"Right," said Mr. Hollister, holding sleeping Sue in his arms.

The search party broke up, but before the children said good night to Aunt Nettie and Bunny, Pam invited them to the party.

"Your grandfather, too," Pete added.

"I know he'd be delighted," Bunny replied, "and so will I."

"I'll be there, too," said Aunt Nettie, "and bring the cider."

"We're going to have a lot of people," Pam said.

"And a lot of cider, too," boomed Aunt Nettie. "Oodles of it."

"Doughnuts, too," said Mrs. Johnson, patting Pam's shoulder. "I'll make them." The children thanked the woman, and Mrs. Hollister promised to contribute ice cream.

While Bunny put Ambrose in the burro's stall, Pete tied Zip just inside the old barn door. He left him a pan of water, some dog biscuits, and Domingo's blanket to curl up on.

"Watch carefully," the boy told him, and Zip woofed softly.

Then Pete ran to join the rest of his family who were already waiting in the station wagon. The children's bicycles had been put in the back.

On the way home, Ricky and Holly fell asleep and woke up only long enough to get undressed and tumble into their beds.

In the morning Mrs. Hollister served stacks of

waffles with plenty of butter and syrup. Ricky and Holly ate triple helpings. "Because we missed supper last night," the redhead said.

At school the Hollisters made plans with their friends to decorate the Johnsons' barn that afternoon. Besides Dave and Jeff, Pete recruited Ned Quinn and Jimmy Cox, who were Ricky's age. During lunch, Mrs. Hollister told her children that Indy would drive them to the farm.

Fifteen minutes after the final bell rang, the excited children were piling into the truck in the Hollisters' driveway. Sue and her mother watched from the front porch.

"Don't forget our five pumpkins," the little girl called.

"Oh, my goodness!" Pam exclaimed. "We almost did!"

She and her brothers raced to the garage for the pumpkins, which they loaded into the back of the truck next to three large cartons marked DECORATIONS and a long flat one labeled SOUVENIRS.

"Yikes," Ricky thought, "I wonder what they are!"

"Is Sue going?" Holly asked her mother.

The little girl and Mrs. Hollister shook their heads.

"We're going to make my costume," said Sue.

"And burn it up again?" Pete asked quizzically.

Sue dimpled while Mrs. Hollister replied, "No, this one we'll keep."

"All set—let's roll!" Indy sang out. The Hollisters swung aboard and the truck backed out of the drive.

The crisp cold air and the Halloween excitement gave all the children pink cheeks by the time they arrived at the farm.

"I'll call for everybody at five-thirty," Indy announced as his riders jumped out. Quickly they unloaded the party supplies, and he drove off.

Holly raced off to pet Zip at the old barn, while Pam helped Ann carry the boxes of candy Mr. Hunter had donated to the party. The boys brought the cartons and pumpkins into the new barn.

"Listen everybody," said Ricky. "I've got an idea about that old Tin Lizzie."

"So have I," Pete spoke up. "Wouldn't it be keen to use it in the Halloween parade tomorrow?"

"Yikes! That's just what I was going to say," Ricky declared. "Can I drive it?"

"Why not?" said Dave Mead.

Ricky whistled and did a cartwheel while the boys argued excitedly about how to get the antique Ford car to town.

"Domingo can pull it," suggested Jeff Hunter.

"Right," agreed Pete, "but we'll have to help him. He's pretty little, you know."

"Then how's he going to pull it tomorrow?" Ann Hunter asked.

Pete grinned. "I've got an idea," he said, and whispered something to Dave. Then the two friends burst out laughing and raced outside. They found Mr. Johnson near the roadside stand, where he had just placed a crate of live chickens.

"The man I sold these to will be along soon to pick them up in his truck," he explained. "What can I do for you boys?"

Quickly Pete told him of their plan for the Tin Lizzie, and waited for the reply with expectant faces.

The farmer thought for a moment.

"Okay. That would be fun, and safe enough if you can blow up the tires. You'll find a tire pump in that barn," he added with a chuckle. "I wish you luck."

The boys raced up the drive toward the old barn, calling to the girls on the way.

But they were too busy to be bothered with an old car. Pam was up on a ladder draping crepe-paper streamers over the rafters as Ann handed them to her. Holly was blowing up balloons.

At one side was a table Mr. Johnson had made from two sawhorses and an old door. When Donna had put a paper tablecloth on it, she began opening big bags of orange and black confetti.

"Don't do that now," said Ann. "It'll spill."

"Donna, you can fill the paper cups with candy," Pam said, "and fold the napkins."

"Let's open the souvenirs," suggested Holly. "I'm dying to know what they are."

"Not until the party," Pam told her. "Why don't you cut out cats?"

"Okay," replied Holly. "But I'd like to have a piece of candy while we work."

"All right," Ann said, "but just one each."

As Holly passed a candy box, Donna blushed. "I've already had two," she confessed.

"Good!" said Holly quickly. "We'll have three to catch up."

"And then no more," Pam warned her.

With a lump of delicious licorice melting in her mouth, Holly drew two huge cats on black cardboard and cut them out. Then she made slanting yellow eyes and pasted them on. She attached the two glaring creatures to posts with thumbtacks.

Meanwhile, Pam and Ann replaced all the light bulbs in the barn with orange ones that Mr. Hollister had provided.

Finally, the girls stepped back and looked over their handiwork. "It needs something spooky," Pam said.

"Like a real ugly witch," Holly suggested.

Pam raised her eyebrows. "That gives me an idea. Come on, Holly!" The sisters hurried out and in a little while were back, carrying a headless dressmaker's dummy and some black clothing.

"I thought Mrs. Johnson might have one of these in her attic," Pam said breathlessly.

"It'll make a keen witch!" cried Donna.

"We'll use one of our pumpkins for her head," declared Holly, and began to draw a face on the largest one. Meanwhile, Pam made a tall, pointed hat out of black cardboard, and Ann and Donna put a long skirt and shawl on the figure.

In a short time, a grinning, snaggletoothed witch stood beside the barn door to welcome the guests.

"Ugh," said Holly happily. "She's horrible."

"She'll scare everybody away," said Donna, giggling.

"Now," said Pam, "we'll make four more jack-o'-lanterns, and we're done!"

Busily, the girls drew faces on the pumpkins and hollowed them out.

"I'm going to make a mean-looking one," Holly said. She frowned, and turned down the corners of her mouth as she worked.

"So am I," said Donna.

When the jack-o'-lanterns were finished, Pam got candle stumps from a supply box and stuck one in each pumpkin.

"Let's put them in a row," Ann suggested.

Two smiling pumpkins were placed on a shelf near the door with the pair of scowling faces between them.

"I'm going to call mine Joey," said Holly with an impish grin.

"And mine's Will," declared Donna. Both girls started giggling.

Suddenly there was a loud thump on the barn door. Pam opened it.

There stood Joey and Will holding a crate!

Holly rolled her eyes at Donna, and stared at

the pumpkins. Donna's plump face grew red as she tried not to laugh.

"We brought some apples for the party," Joey said as he and Will pushed past her.

They put the crate on the floor and bent over it. Quickly Joey pried up the top with his pocket-knife.

"Wait a minute," cried Holly, "that's not—"

Suddenly loud squawks filled the air as Joey and Will dumped the crate on its side. Out flew a dozen chickens. Will flapped his arms yelling, "Cock-a-doodle-do!" and the birds flew around wildly, getting tangled in the streamers.

One landed on Donna's head and she screamed. More chickens flew into the rafters and one crash-landed on the table, flapping up a whirlwind of confetti.

Holly raced outside to call her brothers and Dave Mead, but they were not around. Instead, Mr. Johnson answered the pig-tailed girl's cry for help. He burst into his barn and collared Joey and Will! In short order he scolded the intruders and made them collect the frightened chickens.

"Now, help the girls repair the decorations," he commanded.

The bullies did as they were told, then left meekly, but Pam was sure she heard Joey snicker.

Meantime, Pete, Ricky, and Dave had the old car halfway to Shoreham. While the burro pulled the Ford, Pete and Dave pushed in the back, Ricky

One landed on Donna's head.

and Ned pushed on one side, and Jeff did the same on the other. It was Jimmy's turn to steer.

The boys huffed and puffed when they reached the top of a steep hill.

"Let's stop," Pete ordered. Jimmy steered the car to the side of the road. He hopped out, sat on a slope beside the roadway, and said, "And leave the driving to us!"

The other companions laughed and flopped down, too, while Dave and Pete unhitched the burro, in order to walk him down the hill.

As Dave led Domingo to the roadside, he tripped on a stone and banged into the car.

The Tin Lizzie moved forward.

"Hey!" Pete cried out, and all the boys sprang toward the car.

But old as it was, the Ford had gained speed and headed down the hill.

CHAPTER 17

A SILENT TIGER

"CATCH it!" Pete cried, but the old Ford was picking up speed.

Like a scared rabbit, Ricky ran and leaped onto the running board. The car zigged and zagged as the redhead tried hard to control it.

"Look out!" Dave Mead called from the rear. "Here comes another car!"

Ricky wormed into the driver's seat and stomped on the foot brake. This made his chin touch the steering wheel. But the brake did not work. Frantic, he reached down to pull the emergency brake. It might as well have been a hockey stick!

The boy driver licked his lips bravely, clutched the wheel tightly, and passed the oncoming car, whose driver stared bug-eyed at the lad. But Ricky's problem was not over. At the foot of the hill, the road crossed a narrow bridge. Another car was headed down the opposite hillside toward it.

"I must stop!" Ricky thought. "I just must!" A quick glance over his shoulder showed the other boys racing far behind. The embankment on his right was now a gentle slope leading up to an orchard. The boy made up his mind. Tugging with all his might, he turned the wheel. The Ford shot off the road, up the slope, and came to rest six inches from an apple tree.

"Whew!" Ricky exclaimed, and slid down off the slippery seat.

When the other boys caught up, they slapped him on the back with admiration.

"That was great!" Pete praised his brother.

"Super!" said Dave. Then the older boys ruefully admitted that they had forgotten to test the brakes.

"We'll get Domingo to hold the Tin Lizzie *back* on the rest of the hill," Pete said, and sent Jimmy up to fetch the burro.

In a few minutes the trip to Shoreham was resumed. It was nearly closing time when the adventurers arrived at The Trading Post. A few departing customers gazed in astonishment as the burro pulled the Ford into the alley beside the store and the boys guided it around to the rear entrance.

Pete jumped from the driver's seat and went inside to get his father. "We have a surprise for the parade," he told him.

For a moment Mr. Hollister was too amazed to speak. Then he grinned. "How did you fellows manage it?"

"It wasn't easy," Dave said with a wink at his pals.

Mr. Hollister looked at the ancient tires and shook his head. "It's a miracle you could blow 'em up," he said. Then he helped to unhitch Domingo and load the burro into the station wagon. After driving the boys to their houses, he headed home. When they arrived, Indy was just letting the girls out of the truck.

At the supper table Pam and Holly told about Joey, Will, and the chickens.

Mrs. Hollister laughed until the tears came to her eyes. "That was naughty, but funny," she said. "I hope the poor chicken that crash-landed wasn't hurt."

"Oh, no," Holly assured her. "It only lost a few steering feathers."

"Yikes! Isn't the Ford keen!" Ricky changed the subject. "I'm going to steer in the parade. Could I have a straw hat and a big mustache like in olden times?"

Mrs. Hollister laughed. "I guess we can fix you up."

"How about us?" Pam asked. "Could Holly and I ride in it, too?"

"I was going to be a monster"—Holly spoke up —"but now I'd rather be an old-fashioned girl."

"So would I," said Pam.

After dinner Dave arrived carrying a big bundle. He beckoned to Pete and the two disappeared into the basement. While the other children helped with the dishes, they could hear muffled laughter from below.

As soon as the chore was finished, the girls and Ricky went to the attic with their mother. When they came down, their arms were full of old clothes. Holly was wearing three hats on her head.

The Hollisters paraded into their parents' bedroom where Sue sat on the big bed to watch the others try on the garments. With swift fingers, Mrs. Hollister pinned and tucked them to fit.

By nine o'clock Pam and Holly stood in front of their mother's big mirror in long, pink skirts and blouses with leg-of-mutton sleeves. On their heads were large hats with veils that fastened under their chins. Ricky strutted in long pants, a striped jacket, and a jaunty straw hat.

Mr. Hollister looked in, rolled his eyes, and whistled.

"Wow! Would you look at that! It makes me want to be a Halloweener myself." He promised to get his daughters masks and his son a handlebar mustache from The Trading Post the next day.

Sue bounced on the bed. "Nobody knows what I'm going to be," she crowed.

"And nobody knows what Pete and Dave are going to be," her father said. "The big secret's in our basement and they won't let me down to see it."

Holly was sure she could not wait until the next day. School was out at noon and the parade was to begin at two o'clock in the town square.

At half-past one, Mr. Hollister had Domingo loaded into the back of the station wagon, and old-fashioned Pam, Holly, and Ricky scrambled onto the seats. Just then, Holly let out a squeal as the Hollister front door opened.

Out came a Halloween burro wearing brown shoes and long, cardboard ears.

The body was made of brown cloth and over the head was a burlap bag with big eyeholes. It had a short rope tail which it twirled. Awkwardly, the creature came down the steps and trotted over to the car.

"It's Pete and Dave!" Pam cried out gleefully, as the back end of the burro collapsed and Dave emerged with a big grin.

"Pete and I are going to help Domingo pull the Ford," he said.

"Hah! A pair of donkeys!" Ricky shouted, tipping his hat. Amid the laughter Mrs. Hollister appeared on the porch holding Sue by the hand. The little girl wore a brown leotard with cuffs of leaves at her wrists.

On her head was a huge bunch of colored leaves. She ran to the top of the steps and raised her arms. "I'm a tree!" she called, and the other children laughed and clapped.

"Mommy made my hat and then burned it up so nobody would see it and guess what I was going to be." Sue chattered as she climbed into the car.

"Besides," said Mrs. Hollister, "I wanted to use fresh leaves for today."

"So that was it! Pretty clever," said Ricky, and tried to spin his hat in his fingers.

Mr. Hollister drove straight to The Trading Post and parked behind it. Quickly he went inside and got masks and a handlebar mustache. While the younger children put them on, the two halves of the burro got together. Then, with Sue leading Domingo, they all walked to where the parade was forming.

The giggles and laughter sounded like a hundred kindergarten classes at recess as the colorful ghosts, goblins, and other masqueraders milled about.

Towering above the crowd of costumed figures was a golden-masked witch wearing a high pointed hat.

"That's the one who looked in our window," declared Ricky.

"It's Joey on his stilts," said Pam.

"Crickets, that's a great costume," Pete had to admit. "It might even win a prize."

Right behind the witch was the Ford, which Indy had pushed into place. Mr. Hollister hitched Domingo and his two-boy teammate to the old car, while Pam lifted Sue into the relic. Then, she, Ricky, and Holly took their places.

At the sound of a whistle, the paraders looked toward the judges' stand in the center of the square.

Speaking into the microphone, the chief judge told the children to march once around the square. The whistle blew again and the big shuffle started. Halfway around the square the boy-burro was jostled by an animal trainer leading a tiger on a rope.

"Hey, take it easy," the back end of the burro complained.

Finally everybody halted and the chief judge stepped forward.

"The winner"—he announced in a loud voice —"is the tall witch. The prize is a box of candy donated by the Soda Shoppe."

The winner was called forward. As the witch turned toward the stand, the animal trainer flicked his whip around the long skirts covering the stilts.

With a cry, the tall figure toppled backward! The winner witch sat down hard. Her hat flew askew and the mask slipped off.

"It's Ann Hunter!" screamed Pam. "And we thought it was— How funny!"

Ann burst out laughing at the look on Pam's face. Declaring she was not hurt, the witch lifted her long skirts and walked to the judges' stand.

While she claimed her prize, the animal trainer lifted his mask and made a face at the Hollisters.

"Will Wilson!" exclaimed Ricky. "We might have known!"

"Ha-ha-ha!" said the tiger.

"Joey, too, of course," said Pete. "Look out, tiger, or we'll twist your tail."

A few minutes later the witch was back on her stilts and the parade started down Main Street. At the finish line Mr. and Mrs. Hollister and Indy were waiting. Domingo was loaded into The Trading Post truck and Indy drove him home.

Mr. Hollister, meanwhile, hitched the Ford onto

The tall figure toppled backward!

the back of his station wagon. All the children who could manage, piled into it with Pete at the wheel. The others got into the station wagon, including Joey and Will, who came running at the last minute.

When the odd caravan reached the farm, Mr. Johnson helped Mr. Hollister and the boys unhitch the Ford and push it back to its ramshackle shelter. Pete untied Zip, who bounded down the slope at his side to the new barn.

From the open door came cries of delight from the girl guests as they saw the barn was filled with an exciting orange light.

Mrs. Hollister and the farmer's wife were setting out platters of doughnuts on the refreshment table and Bunny was lining up cider jugs. She called to Pam that Aunt Nettie was coming later with more of them.

Pete and Ricky saw Josiah Applegate putting apples in a big tub of water and ran over to help him. Meanwhile, the girls opened the souvenir carton and passed out tiny flashlights on key chains.

The tiger put out his paw. "Is this all we get?" he asked.

Pam chuckled. "What were you expecting, Joey, a Scout knife?"

"Very funny," said Joey sarcastically, and walked off with his trainer. Although most of the children had removed their masks, Joey still wore his tiger head.

After the second game, Pam noticed that Will

was missing. "That's funny," she told Holly and Bunny. "I hope he's not up to something."

Pam walked up to the tiger. "Where's Will?" she asked. The tiger did not reply. "Listen, Joey," Pam said firmly, "you think you're smart, but I'm going to keep my eye on you."

In ten minutes, however, Pam was having such a good time that she forgot about Joey. Suddenly, she remembered the two bullies and looked around. The tiger was gone, too!

Quickly, Pam told Pete, Holly, and Bunny. "You stay here and keep the party going," Bunny said to Pete. "The girls and I will go look for them."

As the three hurried outside, they saw headlights coming down the old cart road.

"That must be Aunt Nettie," said Pam. "Maybe she saw Joey and Will." The girls ran up the slope and the Jeep stopped in front of them.

Before Pam could speak, Aunt Nettie chuckled. "Girls, my eyes are getting worse all the time! I could have sworn I saw a big yellow pussy-cat walk into that old barn!"

"I'll bet you did see it, Aunt Nettie!" Pam exclaimed. The three excused themselves and raced up to the ruined building.

Pam and Bunny pulled the door open. In the gloom they could make out the tiger, digging in a pile of hay.

"Joey Brill," said Pam sternly, "what are you doing?"

The tiger whirled. Slowly he walked up to the girls, then suddenly pushed past them. He nearly got out the door, but Pam and Holly grabbed his tail.

"No you don't!" cried Pam. "We've got you now!"

CHAPTER 18

THE BACKWARDS COUSIN

PAM and Bunny seized the struggling tiger and held him while Holly unfastened the head of his costume.

"Now, Joey Brill," she said as she lifted it off, "there'll be no more tricks—"

But the tiger was not Joey Brill!

"Mr. Yagar!" exclaimed Pam.

"Yagar indeed!" put in Bunny. "That's not his name!"

"You know him?" chorused Pam and Holly.

Bunny looked disgusted. "He's my cousin, Fred Ragay. You might as well give up, Freddie," she added.

The tiger's shoulders slumped, and Holly raced off to get the others. In a few minutes she returned with her brothers and father, Dave, Mr. Johnson, and Josiah Applegate.

"Crickets!" exclaimed Pete. "That's Joey's tiger suit! How did you get it and where's Joey?"

"Speak up!" said Farmer Johnson sternly.

Ragay swallowed, and explained that he had seen Joey in the parade. "I took him aside and offered him money if he would let me wear the suit at the party. He and his pal in the trainer costume agreed, but insisted on coming to the party first. After a while they slipped out and the Brill boy gave me the tiger suit."

Pam spoke up. "Were you the one I was asking about Will?"

Ragay nodded. "I don't know where those boys are now," he added, "or why they wanted to come to the party first."

"I do," Pam said. "They wanted their souvenirs."

"We know what *you* wanted," Josiah Applegate said to his grandson. "The golden witch."

Ragay could not look his grandfather in the eye. He confessed that he had tried to search the old barn for the witch. "But I was always interrupted," he complained. "Yesterday afternoon the kids were moving the car and running around with decorations. At night it was the dog. I decided the best time to search was when everybody was at the party in the other barn. If anyone saw me in this costume, they'd think I was one of the kids."

Josiah Applegate shook his head sadly. "Freddie, when you were a boy I used to tell you about the golden witch. I never thought you'd try to steal the treasure."

Pete turned to the culprit. "Why didn't you go to Bunny and your grandfather for help? They had the foundry records."

"They did?" Ragay groaned. "I didn't know that. I moved to Ohio long before the factory closed."

"The three of you could have looked for the witch together," Pete went on. "If the rightful owner did not have the treasure already, you could have seen to it that he got it."

"It would have been a good deed," said Pam, "and he might even have given you a share of the treasure."

"I wanted it all," muttered Ragay.

"You always were a greedy boy," Bunny said.

"You ought to be ashamed," put in Pam.

Holly thrust the tiger head back at the culprit and he stood holding it under his arm, his own head hanging.

"You don't know how much I've always wanted to find that witch," he said unhappily. "Two weeks ago, I couldn't wait any longer. I came here and started searching old barns and house roofs. I had to do it secretly so Bunny and Grandfather wouldn't hear about it. I found one witch in Clareton," he added, "but it was the wrong one."

"You searched the storage room at the foundry, too," said Pete.

Ragay looked surprised. "You knew that, too? I thought there might be old records there," he said, then added quickly, "but I didn't take anything. As soon as I climbed in the window, I heard somebody coming and had to go out the same way, fast."

"We were the ones you heard," said Pete. "We reported it to the police."

"Yes, the desk clerk at the hotel told me an officer had checked up on me. That made me nervous, so I moved to a motel and changed my name again."

Ricky grinned. "I hope it was better than Yagar. Yikes, that's Ragay backwards. Pretty corny!"

Ragay winced and went on. "To throw the police off the trail, I turned in my rented car and hired a motorcycle."

Pete and Pam exchanged a look. "Was it you who almost ran into our cart, night before last?" Pam asked.

Ragay nodded. "I didn't mean to do it," he said. "I didn't see you until the last minute, because you didn't have lights."

"But *you* had lights," Pete replied. "Why didn't you have them on?"

"I didn't want to attract any more attention than I could help," the man answered. "I was on my way to the Cobbs' to look for the witch again. I'd been there the night before and climbed up to see if it was lying on their barn roof."

"We guessed that," Pete said, "and also that you were the prowler outside Bunny's house. You heard Pam say that Phineas Cobb had bought the weather vane, didn't you?"

The man admitted that he had.

"What were you doing outside my house?" Bunny asked crisply.

"Trying to decide whether to come in to see you," her cousin replied. "I wasn't getting anywhere in my search for the witch and I thought maybe you might have a clue to it. But I was afraid you would catch on to what I was doing."

Upon further prodding by the young sleuths, the prisoner said that on his second trip to the Cobbs' place he had parked his motorcycle among the trees at the roadside, then crept up to the barn. The sisters had been outside, shooing the hens into their coop for the night.

"The old girls were excited," Ragay said, "and repeated the secret they told you. That's how I knew the weather vane must be somewhere in this barn. And to think I searched it two Sundays ago!" he added.

"You honked the horn then, didn't you?" Holly asked.

"Yes. I had a hunch the vane might have fallen into that old car. I slipped getting into it and hit the horn. I heard someone coming, so I ran away."

"And I'll bet you were that ghostly figure Pam and I saw in the Ford," Dave spoke up.

"Yes," the man replied. "As soon as I heard the Cobb sisters say Adam Cornwall had bought the witch, I took tools from my motorcycle and set out on foot for this barn. I intended to search every inch," he added, "even take the car apart if necessary."

"Pam and I followed you that night," said Dave, "thinking you were Ricky and Holly."

Ragay nodded, "I thought I had shaken you off but I dropped my wrench on the hood of the Ford. That gave me away, I guess, because I heard you trying to open the door. I didn't have time to escape, so I decided to scare you away."

When Ragay had finished, he looked anxiously

from one face to another. "What are you going to do with me now?"

"Turn you over to the police," Mr. Hollister replied sternly. "For one thing, you entered the foundry by a window—without permission."

Ragay turned pale. "Oh, please, I'm not a burglar!" He wrung his tiger-suit paws. "I've never been arrested!"

Pam spoke softly. "He didn't take anything, Daddy."

"He did even worse," Mr. Johnson interrupted, "by nearly causing an accident to you children with his wild driving."

Ragay wet his lips, and looked more pained than ever.

"Well," Pete said, "it's true we didn't have lights, either."

"What about the weather vane he destroyed in Clareton?" Dave asked.

"I'll be glad to pay for it," said Ragay and added hoarsely, "I'm sorry for everything."

Holly pressed close to Pam's ear and whispered, "He looks like a toy tiger with all the stuffing fallen out."

"Sh-sh."

"All right," Mr. Johnson said. "I'll take you to the police station. You tell your story and offer to make good. My guess is they won't be so hard on you."

Ragay agreed miserably.

"Meanwhile, we'll search this barn for the

witch!" declared Ricky. "Everybody at the party can help!"

Holly raced off to summon the guests and Mr. Johnson took Ragay by the sleeve.

"I wish I could stay and help," the man pleaded. "Otherwise I'll never know what the treasure was."

"Let him stay," Pam suggested kindly, and the others agreed.

Soon Holly was back with the excited guests at her heels. Tiny beams flashed here and there as the children searched the ruined barn with their souvenir flashlights.

"Maybe the witch is outside," suggested Ann Hunter, but Pete felt sure it had fallen into the barn when the roof gave way.

Sue tried to dig into the pile of old hay. "I want a tool," she said to Ricky and went away to look for one. A few minutes later she returned and led Ricky to a stall. Sticking up between the barn wall and the back of the stall was an iron bar.

"I need that," Sue said.

Ricky pulled the bar out and Sue beamed her light at it.

"Yikes!" Ricky said. "There's a W on the end! Look! Sue found a branding iron!"

"Don't be silly," chirped Sue. "There aren't any cowboys here."

"That's no branding iron," Pete said. "It's part of a weather vane! Where'd you find it?"

Sue and Ricky showed him. Pete overturned an

"Sue found a branding iron!"

old bucket, stood on it, and beamed his light into the space between the walls.

"Hey! This looks like—it is!" he shouted, and pulled out a dusty metal witch riding a broomstick.

Pam's face glowed with happiness. "Pete! Is it —really?"

Her brother wiped the witch with his sleeve and it gleamed with gold!

"The golden witch! The golden witch!" Holly chanted.

"And Sue found it!" Pam exclaimed. "The prophecy on the tombstone came true!" She hugged her little sister while the excited voices of the guests buzzed around them.

"That's the same bar I nearly pulled out the first day we explored this barn!" Holly said over and over.

Mr. Johnson spoke above the hubbub. "Attention, everybody! We'll take the witch into the other barn and open it. I have tools there."

"I'll do the job for you," volunteered Josiah Applegate. With Pete carrying the witch, the crowd hurried back to the warm, lighted barn and clustered around the farmer's workbench.

While the old foundry worker expertly melted the solder holding the witch together, the Hollisters looked on, their hearts thumping. Ragay managed to squeeze in front of Aunt Nettie to watch.

"Now we'll see," said Mr. Applegate as he put down the hot soldering iron. Carefully he placed the witch on her side and lifted off the top half.

In the crown of her hat lay a compass! At each of the four direction points sparkled a jewel— diamond, ruby, emerald, sapphire.

A chorus of "Oh's" and "Ah's" rose from the onlookers and Pam carefully picked up the treasure.

"How beautiful!" she exclaimed.

"So it was a compass, after all!" exclaimed Holly.

Pam turned it over. "There's an inscription on the back!" She read aloud: "TO ADAM CORNWALL FROM THE MAHARAJAH OF HIMALAYAPORE."

"I bet he gave it to Adam for saving his life," Ricky put in. For those who did not know, he told about the newspaper clipping in Adam Cornwall's scrapbook.

Pam handed the compass to Mr. Johnson. "You are the rightful owner," she said, "because it was on your property."

The farmer smiled. "But you Hollisters found it by your good detective work. You're going to have some reward. How about the golden witch?"

"That's a good Halloween present," his wife added.

Sue clapped her hands. "Daddy can put the witch on the top of our garage where everyone can see her!"

"A great idea!" boomed Aunt Nettie. "Three cheers!"

As the hip-hip-hurrahs rang out, Mr. Johnson escorted sad-faced Ragay out of the barn. The Hollisters followed to the door and looked after the tall farmer and the downcast tiger trudging beside him. When the two disappeared into the darkness, Pete and Pam turned back into the barn. Holly and Ricky started to close the door.

Just then, they heard a noise near the chicken run. In the gloom they could see two figures coming closer.

"Hi," came Joey's voice timidly.

Holly put her hands on her hips. "You're not coming in, Joey Brill—or you either, Will Wilson."

"Aw, we're sorry," said Will. "It's no fun out here in the cold."

"Wait a minute," Ricky spoke up. "I think we ought to forgive them."

"We–ell—all right," Holly said.

Ricky opened the door wide. "Okay, fellows," he said. "Come on in and duck for apples."